Big Mac

by

USA Today Bestselling Author

Dani Haviland

Book Description

Fate and science said they should never have met but after that first touch, he knew he'd stay with her forever. Would the sudden appearance of the father he never knew be their doom?

Chapter 1

April 2015
Greensboro, NC

"Watch out! Here comes another one!" the skinny onlooker shouted, his arms spread wide in a gallant attempt to protect the giant-sized couple as they passed in front of the tavern entrance.

"What's going on?" Benji asked, pulling his wife close to shield her from the unknown impending peril. He heard the winded *thunk* of a body blow come from inside and looked back to make sure his petite protector was also out of harm's way.

"Agh!" A sun-wrinkled cowboy grabbed air as he flew out the door, trying to find something or someone to hold onto before the ground rose up to kiss his face. Unable to find anything to slow his fall, the human projectile wound up performing a hands-free face plant on the concrete curb, a loud crunch indicating his graceless landing had earned him a broken nose. Two seconds later, his cowboy hat parasailed out the door, landing just inches from his head.

"Thirty-seven!" a voice boomed from inside the bar. "Anyone care to make that thirty-eight?"

"Yeah! I do, ya big red-headed nig...aach!"

Another man – this one even bigger than the first – stumbled out the door backward, his feather and snakeskin-banded ten-gallon hat clutched to his chest with trembling hands.

"Thirty-eight!" announced the same, deep voice, accompanied by a chorus of cheering bar patrons.

"Do ye need help?" Benji asked, extending his hand to the marginally conscious Calvin Klein cowboy. The stunned man had landed hard on his rump, his portly belly covered by a belt buckle as big as his face but only half as shiny.

"Uh, no, no thanks," the embarrassed drunkard stammered, his head tipping back to gawk up at the six-foot seven-inch redheaded man. He added, "er...sir," then stumbled away, quickly checking over his shoulder to be certain no one had followed him out of the bar. He staggered to his emerald-green lifted Chevy pickup, then clung to its short bed for support. Continually looking behind him, he fumbled with his bundle of keys, hoping to make a safe and discreet escape. That was the last time he'd ever make fun of anyone with red hair.

"Sir?" Benji repeated the man's stuttered salutation under his breath. "Me a sir?" They were the same age – well, at least biologically. He glanced over and saw his tall wife looking down at the other ejectee, still belly to the pavement, one shoulder up, his hand covering his bloodied nose.

"Are you all right, sir?" Jane asked, concerned for his health, but unsure if she should offer a hand to an unknown white man.

"Ugh," he groaned and rolled over onto his back, then grunted loudly as he struggled to sit up. He lifted his head and saw it was a very dark-skinned woman who had asked about his condition. "Agh!" he screamed, scrambling to his feet. "I swear, I'll never say that N-word again!"

"What's going on here?" Benji asked, scanning the crowd that had gathered to watch the kerfuffle, looking for someone willing to answer him.

"There's a really big dude in there who really, really hates," Benji and Jane's slim wannabe guardian said, then hesitantly whispered, "the 'N' word."

"The 'N' word?" Jane asked Benji in a soft whisper.

Their reedy and gregarious new friend – still reeling from too many drinks – grabbed onto Benji's arm for support. "Yeah, someone called him a red-headed n...n..." He gulped, then blushed when he realized how dark the woman next to his human lamppost was. "Maybe you better 'splain it to her," he told Benji. "I don't wanna chance him hearin' me say it then makin' me number thirty-nine. I don't like that word neither."

"Janie, do ye want to wait out here or go in the tavern with me?" Benji asked.

"I'd rather go with you. I don't know what's happening in there, but I want to see who sounds so much like you." She looked at the man hanging on to Benji's other side. "Are you coming?" she asked and winked.

"Yes, ma'am! I wouldn't mish this for the world!"

The super-tall duo plus one tag-along walked into the bar single file, Benji leading the investigation. "Who's throwin' the trash out into the street?" he asked lightheartedly.

It was obvious who it was, though. The giant-sized man at the dartboard, poised to throw, had a marigold-red Afro hairdo. He turned and frowned at the newcomer interrupting his shot. "Who's asking?" he growled.

"Jest someone who appreciates the housecleanin'," Benji replied and approached with hand extended in greeting.

"Oh, I get it," Jane said softly, noticing that despite having hair every bit as red as Benji's, the young man looked to have African-American ancestors.

"Do I know you?" the bigot-bouncer asked Benji, stalling before committing to a handshake. "You look familiar."

Benji shook his head slowly in answer. He had the same feeling, though. "Do I ken yer family, yer father maybe?"

"I doubt it," the curly-haired man said. "He was gone before I was born. Didn't even leave me his name. Branded me a bastard." He spat on the ground out of habit with the 'b' word, then blushed – there was a woman present. "Sorry 'bout that, ma'am," he apologized, nodding to Jane. "I shouldn't cuss in front of ladies. My mother reared me better than that."

"Apology accepted," Jane said. "I'm sure she's proud of you."

"Well, maybe she was." He paused, then winced. "She was gone by the time I was ten; said I was her pride and joy, her baby boy. Sorry, I didn't introduce myself. I'm called Big Mac."

"Benji MacKay. This is my wife, Jane."

Big Mac squinted his blue eyes and asked, "MacKay?"

"Aye, I'm from a long line of MacKays. Janie here, my wife, has only been a MacKay for a few months."

"MacKay's my mother's name. She used to say she was from a long line of MacKays, too." Big Mac looked from Benji to Jane, trying to visualize his mother. He always thought he'd never forget her face. He didn't have so much as a snapshot of her but did his best to keep her image in his head. For fourteen years, he'd traced the lines of her brows, jaws, eyes – even her ears – in the air, remembering their quiet evenings together, reading or playing Scrabble, before she disappeared. Now her face was fuzzy. This woman before him was much darker than she was

3

but otherwise looked a lot like Mama. Too much like Mama. Suddenly, his mental portrait of his mother was twisting and fading into Jane's face. They were becoming the same person.

"Hey, is he your coushin or nephew or shomethin'?" the drunk at Benji's left side asked. "Cause he sounds like *you*," and poked Benji in the ribs, "but looks like *you*," and pointed to Jane. "Except he has your hair. Well, except for the curly part; that's more like yours…except yours is longer and prettier."

"Thank you," Jane replied. "I think we need to go outside for some fresh air. Would you care to join us, Big Mac?"

Both big men were stunned. They were having a stare-down without animosity – curiosity consuming all of their concentration. "Come on, guys, this is getting intereshting," the sot said, tugging on the men's shirtsleeves, trying to help Jane get them out of the bar.

Both big men turned to the skinny man who reeked of stale cigarettes and beer, then glared at him with identical scowls of intimidation. "Whoa! You *gotta* be related!" he bellowed, too drunk to realize that he was irritating both men whose combined size was about ten times his.

"Out, now, please?" Jane asked softly, trying to avoid making the ado any bigger than it already was.

"Hey, Randy, clear out the patio for me and my friendsh, will ya?"

The bartender looked at his wife's brother then the two big men he was standing between. He hadn't thrown out the younger one who had either punched or kicked out a steady stream of loud-mouthed bikers and drugstore cowboys over the past week – he was glad to be rid of them – but now the tall mixed-blood man was having a staredown with someone nearly his size. No damage had been done to the premises in the last week but having *two* redheaded bulls in his stein-shot-and-wineglass establishment would be pushing his luck.

"Here, Sander, it's all yours," the bartender said and handed him the key. "Just don't get between those two. Cheryl would never forgive me if something happened to you."

"Sure, sure," the happy drunk said, his arms crooked in the elbows of the two behemoths. "Let's take these two gentlemen to my parlor, shall we, ma'am?"

"We shall. This way, gentlemen," Jane said.

The two men were still frozen in their private, silent summit. Jane didn't have to look around to see that they were now the center of attraction in the bar. "Drinks on the house!" she announced with false bravado, repeating the words she'd heard in 'North to Alaska.' And just like in the old John Wayne movie, everyone went to the bar, distracted from the spectacle of the two brooding giants by the allure of free alcohol.

"Sander?" she asked, hoping she had heard his name correctly. He nodded deeply and grinned in acknowledgment. "Would you come around here and help me? I think all they need is a nudge in the right direction."

She was right. The gentle push from behind startled the pair enough that they came out of their mutual trance. Big Mac realized his little buddy was at his side. "Sander, go get us some drinks, will ya? I'll have the usual. What's your poison?" he asked Benji.

"I'll have whatever beer's on tap and my wife likes iced coffee, no cream or sugar."

"Whoa! Did you hear that, Big Mac? She drinks the same stuff you do!" Sander paused, then snorted, "Hmph! Don't see how anyone in hiss right mind…" Big Mac and Benji both frowned at the mouthy man, stopping his words with their glares before his sentence was finished. Sander quickly changed his attitude and tactic. "You know, that musht be a mighty fine drink. I'll have to try it shometime." Then he was gone, his waiter duties offering him a chance for another free beer from his oversized benefactor.

The silence was uncomfortable for all three. The chatty little man was gone now. The only sound was the twang of an old Loretta Lynn song coming from the vintage jukebox. Big Mac broke the tension with an odd, opening question, "What year were you born?"

"Me or her?" Benji answered. He was uncomfortable lying. Dancing around the truth was okay – it was actually fun – but he had just been asked a direct question he didn't want to answer.

"Either one," Big Mac answered with a steely stare at Benji, glancing at his tall wife then back to the tall, amiable redhead.

Big Mac loved his mother dearly – God bless her wherever or whenever she was – but her stories about her parents were too fantastic for him to believe. Well, he had believed them when he was younger, much younger. However, when he bragged about his heritage in the first

5

grade, he had been shamed, humiliated, and made the butt of rude jokes and made-up stories that besmirched both his and his mother's characters. No, he wouldn't – couldn't – believe his mother was a liar, nor that she would intentionally embarrass him. She had, after all, told him never to repeat the story of his family's history. Yes, for now, he'd cast out this one flimsy question to the man whose wife looked so much like Mama. It could be that Mama's stories were true – but he wasn't sure whether he wanted them to be or not.

"I don't know," Jane answered truthfully. "When were you born?"

Big Mac snorted then realized he was rude by answering her direct question with a pressurized nasal discharge. He bypassed an apology and instead turned to Benji. "Do *you* know when you were born?" he asked sarcastically.

"Aye, I do. And do ye?" Benji replied and crossed his arms in defiance. He huffed and said, "Ye ken, we can do this all night, answering questions with questions, but that doesna get us anywhere. Ye tell me first, and then I'll tell ye." Benji looked up and saw Sander trying to open the door into the patio, his hands loaded with three frosty drinks. "And make it fast unless ye want a witness."

Big Mac glared but remained mute, his eyes demanding that Benji answer first. "Okay," Benji sighed, "1771. And ye?"

"2033." He snorted and shook his head in disbelief. "I think we have a lot to talk about...*Grandpa.*"

Chapter 2

"Who are you? I mean, really?" Benji asked.

Big Mac stared at his inquisitor but ignored the question. His bright blue eyes squinted as he examined the face of the man in front of him. He took a deep breath and nodded. "Yes. I see why she said I looked like you." He snorted and added, "Grandpa."

"Why do ye keep callin' me 'Grandpa'? I have no children – ahem, yet – so how can I have a grandchild? I don't think I'm old enough to even be your father."

"Oh? And what year did you say you were born in, old man?" the caramel-colored man asked with a snide chuckle. "I'll bet you're at least one, maybe two hundred years old – by the calendar."

Benji and Jane both gasped at the tall man's words and his intense glare. It was as if he was studying their classified biographies, deciding whether he should arrest them or nor. Jane recovered first. She pursed her lips, determined, then shook her head. "Let's say for a moment that we *are* your grandparents. By the arch of your eyebrows and shape of your ears," she leaned in for a closer look, "I'd say it *is* possible you and I are related. I mean, you could be my descendent... Or, rather..."

Jane shook her head again. The ability to travel through time had skewed and complicated all she knew about biological ages and relationships. When she met Benji's grandfather, he looked to be about the same age as he was. Maybe something like that had happened here, too. Since there didn't seem to be a logical way to figure out this conundrum, she'd see if she could get an answer to her other burning question.

"So, how did you know where to find us?"

"That museum. The pattern on that African cloth in the window is the same as was on your mother's dress. All you had left of her was a scrap from it; the rag you used to bind your hair when you were a slave. She was from Mali. Well, so were you; you were born there, too. You didn't know that, though, did you, until you saw that display?"

Jane's head shook back and forth slowly.

Benji straightened up. "Go on. Whose child are ye, then?"

7

"Your daughter, Mali's. Just moments ago, you decided that if you had a daughter, you wanted to name her Mali. Grandma just told you she was pregnant, right? But you already knew that didn't you? Grandpa."

"I have to tell ye, hearin' ye call me Grandpa is a bit unsettlin'. I mean, I'm not even a father yet…"

Benji and Jane stared at each other but said nothing. They both knew he was a father, but only in the biological sense. Benji had unwillingly and unknowingly sired a child under threat of the mother's life. The issue of that union, a boy, had been adopted by his friend, Billy Burke Melbourne and his partner, Peter Anthony, before he even knew of the boy's existence. Now he was in the child's life, but solely as his godfather.

Big Mac acknowledged his words, slowly nodding his head, then cleared his throat in acceptance. "Well, I guess you're right. The other Mac – Mac Melbourne – is your biological son, but you were never his daddy. At least, so I was told. You were a good daddy to Mom, though. At least for as long as she stayed around…"

"Yer not makin' any sense, lad. We're havin' a daughter?" Benji pulled Jane closer to him, inhaled deeply, and relaxed into her.

Jane didn't cozy into his hug, though. Instead, she tensed, her eyes blazing with maternal fire. "I'd never leave my daughter. But you're wrong, sort of. I haven't told him yet that I'm pregnant."

"But you are, right?" Big Mac asked, his eyes wide, suddenly unsure of his assumptions.

He knew the story. He'd heard it many times over. In his head. He'd only heard the story from her once but had replayed it over and over again. On infinite repeat. It still echoed in his mind silently. Could he have remembered it wrong?

Jane snorted. "Yes, I'm pregnant, but this isn't how I wanted to tell my husband." Her eyes lit up as joy replaced her indignation. "So, you're my grandson, the son of my… Of our," she relaxed into Benji and smiled, "daughter. Mali. Yes?"

"Yes." Big Mac didn't flinch. He didn't smile, but couldn't find a frown, either. He wanted to be angry, but all he felt now was fear. *Could they help him find his mother? And that bastard of a Norwegian time traveler who had sired him?*

Chapter 3

"So, tell me," Benji said, hoisting his stein of beer in salute to the man who could be his grandson, "how did you come to be here and now? Were ye truly seeking us out and if so, why?"

"Why not? Isn't that what you did less than a year ago? Didn't you travel back in time to seek out *your* grandpa?"

Benji reddened at the remark. He hadn't realized until the young man said it that they had indeed both done the same thing. "I guess it's a family tradition then, aye?"

"I think everyone wants to seek out family eventually. My reasons were twofold. One to meet the grandparents I'd never meet otherwise, and two, to see if you could help me find out what happened to my mother."

Although their words had been civil, the tension between the two was tight, ready to pop into an argument with a wrong word or misspoken phrase. Both men knew it and were now mute.

"Excuse me for a moment, Big Mac," Jane said, breaking up their awkward pause. "Why would you never meet us otherwise? I mean, didn't you know the older version of us?"

"No," Mac said, scowling, obviously unwilling to elaborate. He clenched his freckled fists together in front of him, holding them tight as if to keep from striking out.

Benji took a deep breath and sat up straight, his shoulder blades pulled close to gather even more air and fortitude. *He knows of some ill fate or misfortune that befalls Janie and me. He canna say what, but he wants to avert it.* He glanced over at his wife and saw the flicker of realization in her dark brown eyes as she came to the same conclusion. Her jaw slackened, ready to say more, then closed. Yes, some questions were better off not asked.

"So," Benji said, "if ye canna or willna speak of our," he nodded to Jane, "future selves, can ye tell us what ye suspect happened to yer mother?"

"She left in '32 with my father. Or should I say that sperm-donating charmer? It was a good thing he left, too, or you probably would have killed him. I know I would have if a man had taken off with my seventeen-year-old daughter."

9

"Where did they go?" Jane asked with feigned coolness, trying to keep her anger from showing.

Benji's face was scarlet again, his jaws clenched tight in anger at his unborn daughter being defiled. He put his hand up to pause the conversation. "First, tell me. Did she love him?" His shoulders slumped and his eyelids closed halfway in sorrow. "Or did he force himself on her."

"Oh, I'm sure she was at least fascinated with him. I don't think he did anything she didn't want him to. My mom was always a tough one. She was every bit your daughter in size, too. I got my zero-tolerance attitude about prejudice and ill manners from her. Not that I ever knew her to forcibly eject anyone from a bar or any other establishment, but she was always the first in line to defend someone's rights, or to protect those who couldn't fend for themselves. She was a class act when it came to advocacy. She used her wits, not her fists. As far as loving him," Mac shrugged a shoulder, his fists unclenched and parted as he relaxed with his new companions, "I think she was too young to know what it was. As I said, he was gone before I was born."

"And he never came back?"

Mac chuffed in derision. "Yeah, he did. I was about a year-and-a-half-old. He saw her at the park. He wanted her to come with him, plying her with the inside scoop on some future major world event they could drop in on. She said she couldn't bring me into chaos like that. He tried to convince her that I'd be fine if she left me where I was. I guess he took one look at me, grinned at my size and bright red hair, and said I was a cute kid. 'Leave him there. Someone will take him. He'll find a good home with looks like that.'

"Of course, Mom flared up immediately. I'm sure she called him a few appropriate names – although I'm sure they were inappropriate for a public park – and that was that. She told me later she was glad she had the closure. It was fortunate that he wasn't in my life. 'Better to have no paternal influence than a bad one,' she said."

"Geez! She hasn't even been born yet," Benji said, looking down at Jane's belly, "and I already love her."

"Yeah, she was easy to love. She had dozens of friends everywhere we went. Folks were usually standoffish at first – her being so tall and all – and then she'd start talking and have them chilled out in no time."

"Chilled out?" Jane asked.

"Relaxed, calmed down," Benji explained to her. He looked over at Mac. "So, you do know yer granny was a slave in 1783 America less than a year ago, right? She still has a lot of colloquialisms to learn."

Mac squinted, trying to see the woman in front of him in a different light. She was poised and well-dressed but not very confident. That was only when it came to some modern words and phrases being used, though. "I guess you were in the 18ᵗʰ century just a short time ago, weren't you? Did they treat you poorly?"

Jane snorted in derision. "Whipped, beaten, kicked, starved, and given nothing but rags to wear and vermin-infested straw to sleep on..." She took a deep breath, then shook her head as she let it out. "It's hard to believe that it was such a short time ago. The scars on my back are fresh but from the look in your eyes, you don't doubt me. You're just fascinated that you're a descendant of a slave."

"Two slaves," Benji said, a wry smile on his face. "Slavery is still in the world today. Skin color doesna make much difference to those looking to make money with someone else's body, whether using their strong backs for labor or their young flesh for other means."

"Yeah, unfortunately, slavery doesn't seem to go away, at least in the near future," Mac said with a grimace.

"And your mother?" Jane prompted, eager to hear more about her unborn child.

"Tall, amiable, a protective person to all she met, eager to be an advocate to anyone needing comfort or shelter..." Mac's smile grew as he remembered the stories about all the foster children Granny and Grandpa had taken in during the COVID Pandemics of the '20s. "She learned it all from you two. So, now that I've met you and possibly ruined a timeline by popping in a few minutes too early, how about I take off? Oh, and point you in the right direction to that African display outside the museum up the street. Grandma will have a chance to see the cloth, find out she's from Mali, and let you know that Mom's coming."

"Well, it's good to know it's only one," Jane said. "After seeing Evie with triplets and your great-grandmother with twins, I think I'd rather have one at a time."

"Yeah, well, the twins come later," Mac said, then slapped his mouth. "Oops."

"Ye ken, it doesna make a difference if ye tell us how many children we have," Benji said, hoping he'd hear more about his future progeny.

"Yes, I'm curious, too," Jane said. "And are they all healthy?"

"Yes, all are hale and hearty as far as I know. You gather up a few strays later on." Mac looked at his watch and verified the date and year. "Just make sure you keep a year's supply of durable foods, medicines, and toilet paper on the farm. You never know when the world will turn upside down."

"Aye, but by that remark, I take it ye ken."

Mac shrugged a shoulder at his grandfather and smirked. "Forewarned is forearmed. Take care." He stood and looked toward the dozing Sander, propped up against the wall near the patio door, his drink precariously held in one hand. He took two long strides and rescued the glass, setting it on the table.

"Wait!" Jane called out and rushed to his side. "You can't go yet. You didn't tell us anything about where she went and what that spunk donor looked like."

Mac leaned toward her ear and whispered, "Sperm donor. They both mean the same thing but one isn't used in polite company."

"Oh, I'm sorry…"

"No worries. We're family…" Mac said, then groaned in frustration. "I guess I can't just sprint out of your lives now, can I?"

"We'd rather you didn't," Benji said, coming to join them. "Can't we look for your mother together and just say we're kin? I mean, that isna lying. Say, how long have ye been *here*?"

"You mean *now*?" Mac asked, once again answering a question with a question, this time with a big grin.

Jane and Benji both nodded, then looked to Sander to make sure the amiable drunk was still asleep.

"Just a few days this time," Mac said. "Come on, I'll tag along with you if you don't mind. That way I can make sure you find the museum. It seems to me there was one version of the story where a stranger had come up to Granny and Grandpa, telling them about an exhibit in town they might be interested in. I never thought that person would be me, though."

"And that's why I'd like yer companionship. There could be bits of information that may not seem important enough to tell us that are meaningful; something we might otherwise overlook."

Mac looked back at the table where they had all been seated, their glasses still full. "Let's finish our drinks before we leave this fine establishment," he said. He looked at Jane and grinned. "So, you're the one I get the love of iced coffee from, eh?"

Jane reached up and put a gentle hand on his cheek, then looked back at Benji. The two men were so much alike in build and stance. From behind and with long sleeves, gloves, and hats, they'd be indistinguishable from each other. "There are so many things I'd like to know about you. Let's not part ways in a hurry. You have a lot of family to learn about."

"They're fairies, too," Benji whispered

Mac laughed heartily, then looked around. Other than the dozing Sander, they were the only ones on the patio. The jukebox music was so loud in the main bar, nobody could hear them nor did they care what was being said. They were all involved in their own conversations. "Me? I'd say I'm an awfully big fairy."

"One of at least four this size," Benji said, thumping his chest. "As yer granny said, ye have a lot of family to learn about."

"All right. Let's at least stay long enough to finish our drinks. Then we really do need to go to the museum. There might be something there we all need to see."

Chapter 4

The three sat down and nursed their drinks for half an hour, Benji filling Mac in on his heritage and relatives from Scotland and Australia. "You mean there's another six-seven time traveler?" Mac asked.

"Size really doesna have anything to do with it. For us, it is this wee token and visualizing where we want to be." Benji pulled up on the chain around his neck and showed Mac the ancient Greek drachma drilled with two holes. "This is the one that brought yer granny and me back. We were able to use it to send Big Jim, Jane, and me back and forth to 1788 to visit James Melbourne." He fingered the coin one more time, then put it back down the neck of his shirt. "Mighty powerful little token."

"Yes, it is," Mac said. He held up his watch for Benji to see. "It even works when under polycarbonate. That's the real deal under the crystal of my watch."

"Well, I'll be," Benji said, inspecting it.

Jane stood up from the table, too frustrated with the lack of information pertinent to her daughter to sit still. She realized that a year ago – when she was in 1782 – this bold action of getting up without being told to or excused would have earned her another lashing. Her whole body warmed with a flush of relief and comfort, remembering that she was here in the 21st century and married to a man who'd protect her if she couldn't take care of herself. "Stand up, Mac," she ordered using the same tone she'd heard Benji's grandmother use on him.

Both men stood up.

"I meant Big Mac," she said.

Benji smirked, looked straight across at his grandson who was the same height as he was, then winked and sat down.

"Come here and give your granny a hug. I have the feeling you don't plan to stick around too long after we're done here."

A tear welled up in Big Mac's eye, an unfamiliar feeling for the young man who had worked for the past fourteen years to harden his heart. He tentatively wrapped one arm around her back and patted gently. When he felt her head rest into his shoulder and pull him close, he lost it. His shoulders heaved in sobs at her nearness. Her comfort was true and pure, unlike any he'd felt in over a decade.

"You even smell like Mom," he said through sniffles. He saw her look of confusion, wiped his nose with the back of his sleeve, and added, "And that's a good thing."

Benji watched the pair, seeing so much of himself in the young man that a chill ran down his spine. "My family."

"But we're still missing one very important member. Let's go to that museum now," Jane said.

"Sure enough," Mac said, then paused and added, "Granny." He kissed her on the forehead. "I'm so glad I found you."

"Two down and one to go," Benji said.

"Um, yeah. If you say so," Mac said, then looked over and saw Sander was rousing. "Let's get out of here before someone starts asking questions we don't want to answer."

Jane looked at Benji, an unspoken question in her eye. "Later," he whispered. He'd seen that Mac was hiding something, too. There was more than one person they were looking for. Who else had gone missing?

***

"Here's the museum," Mac said, nodding to the window ten feet away from the entrance. The place was locked down for the evening but that didn't matter. What they were looking for was on display.

"Oh, my..." Jane crooned, reaching out to touch the glass. "It's identical..."

"I doubt they'd let you touch it," Mac said, biting off the name Granny. "It is inspiring, though, isn't it. Bright and colorful and full of life."

"Like my mother. I was her only babe, but she is the reason at least six other children lived. She was a wet nurse to the owner's wife and one of his mistresses." She snorted in derision.

"They're all dead and gone," Benji reminded her. "I mean, the bad ones are all dead and gone."

"My mother is, too," Jane said, a faraway look in her eye. "That's all right, though. She was gone before I came here. I would say I hope that the slave owner and all those who treated us so miserably had died a painful death, but I'd rather not think of the past at all. My new family is here." She patted her belly. "And here," and put her hand on Mac's shoulder.

15

"So, ye were born in Mali," Benji said. "M-o-l-l-y is the common way to spell that name, but I have the feeling she'd embrace her heritage and want to spell it like the country. M-a-l-i. Yes, I like it."

"I do, too. Looks like we might want to hurry up and get our new home picked out." Jane turned to Mac. "I hope you're going to say we find a place not too far from here. I really do like the Greensboro area."

"Where are you staying?" Mac asked. "If you'd like, tomorrow I can show you a few sites for sale around here. I'm curious to see if you pick out the same place."

"We're at that motel right there," Benji said, pointing to the building one block away. "And aren't ye playing with fate or something by shopping for land like this with us?"

"Not as far as I'm concerned. As I said, I've been here for a few days. I checked out a few properties in this vicinity. Not that I was going to buy the old homestead before you had a chance to get to it, but to see what it looked like before you rehabbed it."

"Rehabbed?" Jane asked softly.

"Rehabilitated it. Remodeled it," Benji said. When he could see that she was still confused, he said, "Fixed it up so it was better."

"Well, why didn't you just say so," she said, then giggled. "I guess rehabbed is quicker. I'm learning."

"I think yer also getting tired and a bit giddy. Let's walk back to the motel." Benji looked at Mac, hoping his distrust wasn't showing. "What time would ye like to pick us up in the morning?"

Mac looked at his watch again, saw it was only nine-thirty, and said, "I'm an early riser but there isn't much we can do before seven. How about if I pick you up at eight?"

"Make it seven-thirty and we can break bread together."

"Toast and coffee sound great. See you then. Grandpa," Mac said with a wink. "I'm glad I caught up with you."

"If ye remember right," Benji said, "it was us who bumped into ye. I'd say we have a bit of destiny going on."

"Whether it was destiny, fate, or 'planning to at least be in the same neighborhood on the same day,'" Mac said, "we did indeed find each other."

Jane held her arms out boldly, copying the same gesture she had seen her other female family use in Scotland and in 18th century North

16

Carolina. Mac walked into them and gave her a big squeeze. She returned the hug and whispered, "Thanks, Grandson."

He paused a moment, enjoying the familial embrace. This was the closest he'd been to his mother in fourteen years. And she wasn't even born yet.

***

He knew they weren't expecting him for another hour, but he was too antsy to stay in his room. He hadn't told them the night before that he was staying in the same motel. He waited until they had a chance to get settled, and then circled back, parking a block away so they wouldn't see his rental truck.

By six-forty-five, he was making use of the motel's Continental breakfast buffet. He had already downed his first cup of coffee and was up to retrieve his toast and pour a second cup when he almost walked into him. "Oh, hi, Grandpa. I see you're ready a little early."

"And you've been here since when?" Benji asked.

"Last night." He flashed his keycard envelope with his room number on it. "My home away from home." He poured a cup of coffee for Benji and nodded to a table in the corner.

"I have so many questions to ask ye," Benji said, sitting down. "I think we could be in the same room for a week and I wouldna ask the same one twice. But I'm afraid to speak even one. I dinna want to mix up knowin' ye as a lad with ye bein' a full-grown man."

"No worries there. You never knew me. Last night was the first time we've met."

"There you are," Jane said, coming into the room late. She noticed the change in Mac's looks. "What did you do to your hair?"

The young redhead's bright smile was as broad as his grandsire's. "Oh, this is how I usually wear it: slicked back. I only have it picked out into that wild Afro style when I'm looking for trouble."

"Ye go lookin' for it?"

Mac shrugged and picked up his toasted bagel. He inspected it and decided it needed cream cheese. "I'd been there the day before, waiting. Watching. A few men came in and harassed the bartender and anyone of color or who were of a hefty size. They left, saying they'd be back tomorrow, same time. Randy – the barkeep – said they made the rounds regularly, all up and down the street. I decided they needed a lesson in manners." He peeled open the mini container of white spread and

17

schmeared on the whole works. Holding his food up to emphasize his point, he said, "So, I showed up the next day, too. You know, I really can't abide rudeness or discrimination. Actually, any prejudice, but I've noticed the first blast of bigotry is always based on a person's appearance. I figured if there was any doubt about my ancestry, wearing a 'fro would seal it."

"So, your sire was white. That means yer a quarter African."

"Yup. A quarter Mali, quarter Scot, and half Norwegian time traveler."

Benji leaned forward and whispered, "Yer half Norwegian but one-hundred percent time traveler." He sat back up and saw that Jane was waiting for him to finish. "Yes, coffee and a few of those bagels will be fine. Toasted and with cream cheese, if you don't mind. I can spread my own."

Jane put two bagels in the toaster, then poured more coffee and gathered toppings for their bread. She took a disposable knife from the metal cylinder and inspected it, running her thumb across the top of it. Plastic still fascinated her. She heard the bagels pop up. And electricity. Heat without fire. What would people think of next?

"Here you are. I can get you some eggs to go with this," she offered. "You, too, Mac. Man does not live on bread and coffee alone."

"Ye ken ye dinna have to serve us," Benji said.

"I'm getting mine, so I might as well fill up three plates. I have a feeling that we have a long day ahead of us."

"Whether we do or don't, I am a bit peckish. Fill a plate with eggs and whatever meats they have, if you dinna mind," Benji said. "I'll pass on the pastries for now."

"And you?" Jane asked.

Mac knew she'd heard his stomach grumble. "Sounds good. I'll have what he's having, too, if it's not too much trouble. The farms for sale tour will take a couple of hours, at least. I'm glad I sprung for renting the big truck instead of the economy car."

Benji leaned sideways in his seat and looked at Mac's long legs under the table. "I'd say ye were doin' it fer yerself as well."

"I learned long ago that paying a few bucks extra for plus-size accommodations makes a big difference in comfort. No sore backs from being hunched over." Mac sipped his coffee and watched as Jane served up three plates of bacon, sausage, and scrambled eggs. He put the cup down and whispered, "Just last year? She was a slave in 1783 less than a year ago?"

"Aye, and not too far from here," Benji said. "Oh, and she has verra good hearing."

Jane smiled as she turned toward the two men, balancing the food without a tray, the utensils and paper napkins clenched in one hand. "Overhearing others has saved me a lot of trouble over the years. Tell me, is that a talent you inherited?"

Mac's caramel-colored cheeks blushed. "How'd you know?"

"Just a feeling. Oh, and seeing your eyes widen just a bit more when your grandpa mentioned it. That's more of a talent, though: reading people's expressions."

"I guess I don't want to play poker with you then, do I?"

"Poker?" Jane looked back and forth between the men.

"It's a card game, one where ye bluff – that is, lie – and pretend ye having a winnin' hand of cards when ye don't."

Jane nodded and speared a link sausage. "I'm glad to hear it's not playing catch with fire-tending tools."

Mac laughed unexpectedly and quickly put his hand in front of his mouth full of food. He chewed and swallowed. "And that sense of humor…"

"Aye, I think all the MacKays have it, either born with it or married into it." Benji leaned forward and added in a whisper, "It's a survival skill, ye ken."

"Yes, I do believe it is. Grandpa."

"Excuse me," Jane said, her curiosity overcoming her inherent shyness, "but why do you always pause before saying Grandpa?"

Mac chuckled. "You noticed that? Well, I guess it's because I'm savoring the name. At least, now it is. I was unsure of using it when we first met. The first time or two I said it, it felt like a dig. A jab?" Mac saw her confusion at the words. "An insult?"

"Oh, because you two aren't that far apart in age, at least in biological age."

Mac shoved a big bite of eggs into his mouth and nodded, wanting to end the conversation about his initial rudeness and get breakfast downed so they could hit the road.

What would they find today?

Chapter 5

After breakfast, Jane looked back at the large trash can in the corner, already half-full of disposable plates, cups, and utensils. "Such waste when just a few minutes with a pan of soapy water would take care of it all."

"Welcome to the 21st century," Mac said. "Don't worry. I don't think it's taking away anyone's job."

He led the way to his rental, then opened the passenger door, offering Jane a hand to help her get in. "There's a back seat but when you're sitting up here, you see the countryside and not the back of my head. There's plenty of room; I'm pretty sure we'll all fit."

Cold chills raced up her arms as they always did when she got into a motor vehicle. Jane shook her head, refusing his help. She mumbled, "Thanks, the front is fine. Oh, and I got this." She clutched onto the truck frame with one hand and used the handgrip inside the door with the other. Feeling the sturdy hard metal and plastic strap was more reassuring than holding onto someone she'd just met. And who wasn't her husband.

Benji climbed in after her. Mac started the engine and once buckled in, pulled his smartphone from his inner vest pocket. He looked around the parking lot, made sure no one was nearby, then tapped an icon. A holographic screen projected in front of him, just above the steering wheel, not quite touching the windshield.

"What's that?" Benji asked.

Mac swiped on the corner of the device. "My map among other things. It's compatible with this old technology, too."

"*Old* technology? I dinna think we have anything like that. I mean, I've seen gizmos like that in movies about the future, but I dinna think they had anything out like that yet."

"They don't. I brought it with me. It can use the same digital signals for phone calls that you use. The battery lasts a month, sometimes longer, though." He turned the three by five-inch unit over and the image disappeared into his lap. "There's a solar panel here if I slide the back up. It takes about an hour to charge, though. I only use this when absolutely necessary. I programmed the info on the farms for sale into it." He tapped his right temple. "I have a very good memory, but I didn't want any screw-ups. There's been a little excitement in my life lately and I wanted to make sure I didn't forget the addresses."

"Aye, I guess meeting yer grandparents fer the first time is a bit exciting. I ken meeting my grandson before his mother is even born is still a bit unsettling for me."

"Me, too," Jane said, still watching Mac's face. *The little excitement in your life isn't meeting us. There's something else going on that you're not sharing.* She looked at Benji and grimaced slightly, making sure her face wasn't visible to Mac. Benji replied with a quick narrowing of his eyebrows, and then his general-purpose congenial smile returned. He may not have seen what she saw, but he could tell she had sensed something. There was nothing they could do now but move forward.

"How big are these farms we're lookin' at?"

"Forty acres and up," Mac said, a true smile of contentment coming to his face. He'd never seen the MacKay Manse but had heard about it.

Was it possible that Mom had returned to it and was waiting for him – them – there, right now? He hadn't thought of that when he first arrived three days ago. Had he messed up, meeting his grandparents before scouting the property? A cold sweat beaded on his forehead and breakfast sat hard in his gut. It roiled loudly, embarrassing him.

Benji looked over at Mac, saw his unease, then made a joke to try and lessen the young man's emotional pressure. "Janie, is that mornin' sickness comin' at ye already?"

She patted her tummy, started to answer that it wasn't her, then saw the heightened arch of his eyebrow. "Let's hope it's just a bit of noise from my body, not caring for those powdered eggs. As long as it stays down, we won't have to pull over to the side of the road."

The tension eased in Mac's neck and shoulders at the banter. Yes, his grandfather knew where the belly protests were coming from, but he and his grandmother were trying to make him feel at ease. It worked.

"The first property is just up the road. We can't go in to see the building without a realtor, but we can drive by all these sites without an escort."

"I can tell ye right now, I'll pass on this one. Barns and houses can be repaired or replaced but rerouting the roads coming into and out of a homestead is more work than I care to undertake. If there is some distress comin' to our country, I dinna care to be so close to a busy highway."

"You're sure you don't want to go check it out?" Mac asked, trying to suppress his grin of satisfaction at the quick refusal.

"If the other two are lesser in size than this one, we'll have to keep lookin' for a bigger one. Do ye think ye might have a wrong address? Ye did say ye've never been to the old homestead, right?"

"Right," Mac replied, his smile now wide and not held back.

Jane breathed a sigh of relief. The tension was completely gone, his veil of secrets held now dissipated. "Next place, please," she said, then leaned back into Benji. Content again.

***

"It's just up here. The road ahead's not paved, though," Mac said, glancing down at his holographic image. He swiped his hand in front of the phone's screen, closing the app.

"I'm fine with dirt or gravel roads," Benji said. "Folks don't drive so fast on them. That is, if they even come down them at all. If they do, it generally means they're either local and on their way home or have business or kin to attend to."

"Hmm. I never thought of it like that," Mac said. "It's also at the end of a dead-end…"

Thunk!

The truck lurched forward but didn't stop. It wasn't a mechanical failure or flat tire that had caused the surge. They'd been hit from behind.

Mac grabbed the steering wheel tighter while Jane and Benji reached out and braced their hands against the dash. "What was that?" Benji hissed, looking into the side mirror for another vehicle.

Mac double-checked his side and rearview mirrors while Jane twisted around and looked out the back window. "I don't see anything," she said.

Mac and Benji both growled with the same angry, guttural tone. Jane fought the urge to laugh. Instead, she rolled her eyes and unbuckled, rising from the seat, turning completely around. She moved her head up and down, trying to see through the gap where the tailgate and truck bed met. "I see it! It's a small yellow car. I mean, it's low to the ground. It looks like one of Little Mac's toy cars. I think he said it was a Coramaro."

"Hold on to the lead," Benji said to Mac. "Janie, let me look."

Jane sat back down and huddled close to Mac, giving her husband more room to rise tall in the seat and turn around. "Aye, it's a Camaro,"

22

he said then sat down and buckled up again. "Hang on. I dinna think he's trying to ask directions to the nearest donut shop. He wants to run us off the road."

"Don't worry," Mac said. "Now that I know he's there and plowing into us wasn't an accident, I'm going to switch to offensive driving mode. Damn! Now I wish I'd come yesterday to check out the roads…"

Benji looked back over his shoulder. One arm up, grabbing the handhold above him, he braced the other on the flat dash. "Hold on, Janie!"

Biting off the question, 'To what?' Jane stuck one arm straight up, pressing against the ceiling panel, the other next to Benji's.

"I got this," Mac said. "Here we go…now!" He turned the steering wheel sharply, taking advantage of a pullout for slow-moving tractors at the side of the road.

The low-riding Camaro sped past them and hit the transition where the pavement stopped and the gravel started. *Crunch…kathunk…kathunk.* The lemon-colored one-piece fiberglass bumper and front body panel flew off, spat out by the wide rear tires, flung into the air like an oversized kite, landing askew in the field beside them. The once spectacular vehicle skidded from side-to-side as the driver tried to regain control and keep it on the road. Two hundred feet ahead, the brake lights came on and it screeched to a complete stop. He gunned the engine a couple of times, backed up, braked hard, then pivoted in a tight circle, stirring up dirt and gravel, creating a miniature storm system. The headlights shone at the MacKays through the dust. Like a cocked gun, the car was now pointed at them.

"Um, do ye have this, Mac?" Benji squeaked, both fearful and frustrated that the situation was out of his control.

"Yeah, I do," Mac said coolly. "Do you have a camera on your phone?" he asked.

"Aye."

"Then shoot video now. I want to see who this bastard is. Oops. Sorry, Granny."

Benji pulled out his phone and aimed it at the car. "It's filming," he said.

The antagonist's motor revved one more time, the turbo whining like it was crying for help, then the high-horsepower Chevy came peeling down the road straight at them.

"Hold on!" Mac hollered. Like two powerful magnets being pulled together, the gap between them closed. Glancing to either side, Mac estimated the depths of the ditches, calculating which would be the safest spot to dive into.

Three long seconds later, he turned away from the game of chicken and stomped on the brakes at the same time, sliding sideways onto a service road hidden between the tall rows of corn. He hadn't landed in a ditch but hadn't seen who the other driver was. All he caught was the man's large hand in front of his face, middle finger high, flipping him the bird.

"Did you get the video?" Mac asked.

Benji handed him the phone. "Ch...check it out. I think I'm gonna be sick," he said and opened the door. A half dozen steps away from the truck, Benji coughed a few times, then wiped a bit of spittle from his mouth. "False alarm." He looked up and saw that Jane had followed him out and was ten feet away, losing her breakfast.

"Sorry 'bout that," Mac said. "I know it's a lot easier when you're hanging onto a steering wheel and know what you're going to do next. I didn't have time to tell you. Is she okay?" he asked, nodding to Jane.

"I'll be fine. I think it's a little morning sickness and a lot of terror. Either one would probably have sent breakfast flying."

Mac grinned weakly, embarrassed that he had caused distress but glad they hadn't crashed or landed upside down. He looked at Benji's phone, tapped on the icon, and brought up the most recent shot.

"I didn't have time to zoom in on him," Benji said. "But I guess that could be a good thing. The resolution on this will be better. May I?"

Mac handed the phone back. It had been a long time since he'd held one so heavy and rigid. No wonder the screens were always cracking on them.

Benji tapped and swiped, his eyes wide as he slowly went through the video frame by frame. "Do ye ken any tall redheads?"

"Other than you and me? No. Why?"

"The way this man's shoulders are high in the window, I'd say he's about as big as us."

"White or Black?"

"Oh, he's every bit as white as me." Benji showed the picture briefly to Jane, then brought it back to Mac. "Ye canna see his features for the hand in front of his face, but he's a pale man, fer sure."

Mac held his finger above the image, then remembered that old technology used two fingers to enlarge a picture. Now it was his turn to be wide-eyed. "Does he look like someone you know?" he asked Benji and Jane, now huddled close together.

"Aye," Jane said. "Someone we met last night."

"He's yer sire maybe?" Benji asked.

"Almost like looking in a mirror, my color washed out by bright light. Yeah, I'm pretty sure that's Storm, the Viking time traveler," Mac said, staring at the image, stunned.

"Well, since we're so close and he's gone, do ye want to explore some property?" Benji asked.

Jane shrugged then snuggled close to him. "As long as we do it together."

"What else do we have to do?" Mac asked then reddened as he looked at the cuddling duo. "Oh, is this your honeymoon?"

"Nah. We came here to look fer a place to build a home and start a family. It appears we have the cart before the horse, though. Our family's already started."

Mac took three bottles of water out of the case on the back seat. "Well, if all tummies are settled, let's go see what's up the road."

"I dinna ken what the place looks like, but I like it already. It seems to be alive, keepin' out the riff-raff for us."

"Guard Dog Road," Mac said softly, looking off into the fields of tasseled corn.

"What? Aye, that'd be a good name for it."

Jane nudged Benji. "I think that's what we name it in the future. He slipped." She turned back just in time to see Mac's grin of satisfaction disappear. He'd let something slip on purpose. And it was probably 'again.'

Chapter 6

"I would say you should close your eyes, so you'll be surprised," Mac said, trying to lighten up the anxious mood, "but this is going to be new for all of us." He glanced down at his phone's screen to verify he was on the right heading, then frowned and shook his head.

"Is there something amiss?" Benji asked.

"No, nothing's wrong. I'm just fascinated with this new reality. My mother used to tell me stories about how awesome it was growing up and…" Mac paused, sucking in and biting his bottom lip. *Shut up, fool!*

"And…and," Benji prompted.

"And I don't think I should be sharing memories," Mac said, suddenly dour as he remembered some of the stories Mom had shared of frustrations that had escalated to family feuds about appropriate clothes and whether a teenage girl should wear eye makeup or not.

Trying to ease his obvious insecurity, Jane brought the subject of conversation back to the present. "So, does this mean you might want to stick around? I mean, it would be awkward after she," she patted her belly, smiled, and continued, "after Mali was born. I agree that you two probably shouldn't interact, but we'd love to have you stick around for at least six months."

Mac's eyes were hot as tears started. He hadn't had any family love in so long, he had forgotten how wonderful it felt to have someone truly care about him. Rather than deny her generous offer, he sighed with a wide grin and said, "We'll see."

A soft but rapid 'pinging' from his phone alerted Mac that he was near his final destination. "Look up, folks," he said, smiling. He turned left down the path between two barbed wire fences, overgrown at each post with Johnson grass, the semi-barren spot between the mounds the only indication that there was an actual entrance to the 'MacKay Manse.'

"Oh, my," Jane said. She suppressed a giggle when she saw the look of shock on Mac's face, the complete opposite of the glee on her husband's.

"Well, ye did say it was going to take a wee bit of work, aye?" Benji asked Mac.

26

"Could you forget I said anything? We still have to look at the other site. I mean, I slipped and should never have given you any indication of which property..."

Benji put his hand on Mac's arm, noting the tense grip the young man had on the steering wheel. "All right. Ye have the map on yer phone, correct? Show me the other place of interest. I may be able to tell by its juxtaposition to roads or water whether I like it or not. I can already tell there's either a creek or pond on this lot. At least, ye did say this was over forty acres, aye?"

"Aye," Mac said, subconsciously mimicking his speech. He patted his grandfather's hand, still on his arm, to let him know he didn't need any more emotional support. "And you're right. I can see the greenery down there. The fields are fallow and overgrown with yellow and brown weeds. Those trees are well-watered from a natural source."

"If you don't mind," Jane said softly, a bead of sweat on her upper lip, "I'll let you two check it out first. I'm feeling a bit queasy again."

"Are ye sure?" Benji asked, then realized she wouldn't have spoken up if she wasn't already extremely nauseous. "Do ye want the windows down or the air conditioning left on? It's still a bit warm even if it is early."

"Windows down," Jane said, then suppressed a hiccup with her hand in front of her mouth.

"All right. We'll leave ye to recover. Just hit the horn if ye need me." Benji leaned over and gave her a gentle kiss on the side of the head, then climbed out of the truck. "Morning sickness," he whispered with a broad smile.

The two men walked up the rickety front steps to the broad porch. At least twenty percent of the boards were broken or missing. "Looks like a wee bit of repair is needed," Benji said, then chuckled. "But I do love havin' a large gatherin' area outside and under cover."

Mac looked up at the security lockbox on the side of the screen door. It had been pried away from the frame and the inside door was wide open.

Benji moved in and looked closer at the push-button device. "I'd say this was done recently." He pointed to an area that was wiped clean. He blew on it, scattering dust motes over the once shiny spot. "No fingerprints, so I'd say whoever busted into the place was wearing gloves. No sign of a prybar, so he must have been pretty strong to break this away from the doorjamb."

Mac looked back at the truck, frowning in concern. Jane was leaned back, chin up, taking deep breaths to calm her upset tummy.

"She'll be fine," Benji said as they walked to the house. "If ye stick around a while, I'll tell ye how we met in the 18th century. She's the toughest person I've ever met. And the stubbornest!"

Mac winked at him but didn't say a word, his bright smile speaking for him. *I'd stay just to hear that!* He turned back to the business at hand and opened the screen door, the top hinge pulling away from the wood, twisting the frame. Cautiously peering inside, he listened for sounds of occupancy, letting his eyes adjust to the darkness before walking into the unknown. A small creature skittered across the floor, tiny squeaks marking its unseen path.

"Mice," Benji said. "They'll leave us alone. It's the rats ye have to watch out fer."

His eyes now adjusted to the semi-darkness, Mac led the way. Benji waited a moment to make sure his grandson didn't fall through broken floorboards. One of them had to hang back to rescue the other in case of trouble.

"It looks like someone was looking for something in the library," Mac said. "And very recently." He pulled out his smartphone, whispered, "Alexis, flashlight," and the room lit up.

"Wow!" Benji said, following the path of the light. "Shine it over here, if ye would."

Mac shone it on the rolltop desk, the drawers pulled out, the contents scattered across the floor. Benji ran a finger across one of the papers. "No dust."

"Alexis, infrared light," Mac said. He held the phone up and tracked the faint trail of large footprints heading toward the back of the house. "This way."

Benji followed Mac as they stepped to the side of the prints, not on top of them. Mac paused a moment to take a picture of a glowing print, his foot next to it to show the relative size before it faded completely. He looked ahead and saw they had stopped.

"Where did he go?" he asked.

Benji looked up. "The attic maybe? You and I could get up there without a ladder, but I doubt many people could. It looks like yer sire was here before we were."

"Exactly what I was thinking. Just because he entered this way doesn't mean he exited here. Hold this for a sec, would ya?"

Benji took the phone and shown the reddish light toward the access panel in the ceiling. It was back in place, but handprints were glowing red on two sides. It had recently been removed and replaced.

"Are ye sure ye want to go up alone?"

Mac snorted. "No. I don't care for closed-in spaces, but you and I both saw him leave. Unless there's another tall man or woman prowling the premises, I'd say these prints were about a half-hour old. They disappear faster in the winter. The summer heat is working with us. They may even be over an hour old. Here, let me have that back."

Benji handed him the phone and huffed. He felt helpless. The young man with the futuristic electronics was better at searching out missing objects or people than he was. Mac's fancy smartphone was more like a genius-phone.

"Any luck?" Benji called up after a minute of hearing nothing but mice, creaking walls, and rustling leaves.

"Not really. It looks like whoever it was startled a rat. The rat lost. I'm glad I didn't step in it."

"Still visible in the infrared light?" Benji asked.

"Yup. Would you follow the sound of my footsteps to the outside of the house? I want to see where he exited."

Tracking the sounds through the hall and dining room area Benji wound up in what appeared to be a canning kitchen, complete with outdoor sink and propane gas stove. A crunch sounded, then two quick steps, and then a 'Whoop!' as Mac jumped off the small porch.

"That was close," Mac said, rising to his feet from his crouched landing position. "I thought I was going to fall through."

"And…" Benji prompted from the doorway.

"Nothing. Zilch. Nada. I don't know if he found what he was looking for or not. Of course, it would help if we knew what it was."

"Or who it was," Benji said.

"Nah. I'm pretty sure it was Storm." He held up a twist of long red hairs. "Found these on a nail in the rafters. No kinks or curls, so it isn't mine. Still warm enough to glow red with the infrared light, so it wasn't from a previous inhabitant." He stuffed it in his shirt pocket. "Let me know if you find a bag or envelope around here. I don't want to confuse it with my own DNA."

Honk! Honk! Honk!

Mac ran around the house as Benji sped back through it the same way he'd come in. Both wound up at the truck at the same time.

Jane had company.

Chapter 7

"I'm sorry I frightened you," the distraught man told Jane through the truck's open window. Standing three feet away, he held his hands behind his back, hoping she didn't see him as a threat. His sincerity was obvious to Mac but not her husband.

"Step away from my wife!" Benji bellowed as he strode towards him.

"I'm sorry. I'm truly very sorry," Silas said to him, taking two more steps back. "At first, I thought she was my fiancée. I mean, my friend," he stammered. "Well, I was going to ask her to marry me soon. Very soon. Maybe even this evening." He paused and took a deep breath, oblivious to the rage in Benji's eyes. Instead, he looked over at the dilapidated house in awe. "She said this was the place."

"Who did?" Mac asked, coming closer to step between the confused silver-haired man and his fuming redheaded grandfather. He glanced at Jane and noticed her frustration as she tried to get out of the truck. She was slapping and clutching at the handles and buttons, searching for the right one.

"Just a sec," Mac said to the two men and stepped between them to open her door. He held out his arm, offering her assistance.

"I've never met anyone who looks like me," Jane said, trying to mask her curiosity as she gracefully straightened to her full six-foot-four inches.

Silas gave a half-smile, half-grimace in return. "Your children look like you," he said hesitantly, shrugging one shoulder meekly.

Jane's legs buckled, but Mac was ready and reached out. He pulled her to his side, supporting her as she composed herself.

Mac stared at the stranger, then cleared his throat. "My mother?" he asked, his eyes bright with excitement. Confusion set in and he shook his head. "My mother was here?" he asked himself. Then his indignation and the loudness of his voice grew. "You know my mother?"

Silas's mouth opened and shut, fatigue slowing his explanation about what was going on.

Mac snorted in frustration at not getting an immediate reply. "Well?"

Silas looked at the redhead without the curls to see his reaction.

31

Benji, once angry, had tamped down his rage and replaced it with a mixture of puzzlement and fascination. Now it was his turn to shrug. "What he asked," he said. "Answer him."

"Let me back up a little. Or a lot, depending on how we're measuring *time*," the man said.

Everyone in the group looked back and forth between each other, their unspoken question of 'Are you referring to time travel?' answered by their identical curiosity.

"*When* did you come from?" Mac asked.

"2010. Just a short five-year hop forward. A first for me. Oh, forgive me for not introducing myself. I'm Silas Priest from Massachusetts."

"What are you doing here?" Mac asked, continuing the interrogation.

"Now, before I answer a lot of questions – and I will answer them all," Silas said in his most congenial but no-nonsense tone, "may I have the pleasure of knowing your names?"

"Mac MacKay. This is Benji MacKay and…" Mac paused the introduction when he noticed Silas grinning at his grandmother as if he'd just met a movie star.

"So, it is you, isn't it?" Silas asked her, smiling broadly. "I mean, do I have the pleasure of meeting Jane MacKay?" he asked and picked up her hand.

"Am I supposed to know you?" she replied and stepped back, her hands now behind her.

"I never had the honor," he said, "although I've heard what a charming and beautiful woman you are. Yes, your beauty is beyond description…"

Benji moved in between Mac and Jane, mumbling an 'excuse me' to Mac. He pressed up close to Jane and put his arm around her protectively. "Ye'd better not be makin' a pass at my wife, especially with me standin' right here."

"Oh, I'm so sorry. I think that came out wrong. I haven't slept in nearly forty-eight hours. Julianna and I drove all night and day from New England. When we got here, a car was in front, the motor still running."

"A late-model yellow Camaro," Benji said rather than asked. He glanced at Mac and saw he was shocked. *What's with him? Did I miss something?* He shook off Mac's bafflement and looked to the stranger.

Silas nodded in agreement about the vehicle. "Brand new, I believe," he said. "We parked up the road so we wouldn't be seen. I asked my soon-to-be fiancée to wait in the car while I investigated. I approached the house and saw a tall red-haired man inside, ransacking the place. Not that it was in any great shape to begin with, but his actions were clearly a case of breaking and entering."

"Aye, he tore the lockbox off the front door."

"Precisely. He wasn't aware that I was in the brush, watching him. He was cursing in Norwegian, I believe, clearly looking for something. I moved to the window to get a better look. He must have had some knowledge of the layout because when he got to the kitchen area, he looked straight up and practically flew into the attic. You see, he was every bit as big as one of you."

"Storm," Mac said.

"That's who I thought he was, too," Silas said. "I must have made a noise because I heard his footfalls above me, tossing boxes and such, then suddenly running toward the window. I saw him practically fly out of it, landing on his feet as light as a tomcat."

"Back up a bit," Mac said. "You said you were here with Julianna. Where is she now?"

"I wish I knew. I was on my way to the car to let her know what I saw when you pulled up. I thought I'd hang back and see who else was interested in this old place. My car's gone now. At least, it's not where I parked it. I hope she just moved it so it wasn't visible from the road. Lord, I hope she didn't take off. I don't want to lose her. Again."

Mac raised an eyebrow to Silas, letting him know to be stingy with his explanations about Julianna for now. Silas saw it and answered with a quick glance off to the side. He understood. Benji and Jane didn't know who she was at this point. Too much information about their second daughter could mean trouble.

"If only that burglar had left something behind so I could find out who he is," Silas said, deflecting the conversation from Julianna. *Yes, these three people are definitely Julianna's family – her father, mother, and nephew. She's been searching for her older sister for over twenty years now. Today's the closest she's been to her biological family since she left to find Mali nearly twenty-three chronological years earlier. Now the real question: is my more-than-a-lady-friend hiding from her family, or has that smooth-talking troublemaker, Storm, lured her away, too?*

"Ahem." Mac cleared his throat for a third time, not wanting to be rude to the obviously sleep-deprived man but wanting to let him know he had a DNA sample for him.

"I'm sorry," Silas said, shaking his head. "I think I'd better sit down before I fall down."

"Looks like there are a few barrels on the front porch that could double as stools," Benji said. "Jest watch yerself comin' up the steps."

Stepping over the split or missing wooden planks to the south-facing porch, Benji pulled a few of the empty wooden containers away from the wall. "These should work," he said, dusting off one of them for Jane. "If this is to be our new home, it looks like I have some major remodelin' to do," he said, looking closer at the supporting beams.

Silas arched an eyebrow in Benji's direction. *You've done this sort of thing before, haven't you?*

Benji shook his head and smiled, not in denial but in amusement. *Yer pretty good at talkin' without sayin' a word.*

Silas nodded. *So are you.*

"If you two have finished your conversation…" Mac said, frowning at Silas. "Do you want a DNA sample of the burglar or not?"

"Yes! Of course, I do! It seems as if your dau…" Silas saw the stern look from Mac and quickly began again. "It seems as if my fiancée has been trying to catch up with this Storm person for a long time." He started wringing his hands, remembering that she had either been searching for or running away from the man for twenty years and had now disappeared herself. *Is Julianna really paranoid and I've fallen for a nut? Or is she injured, kidnapped, or in danger and I'm just sitting around here, babbling like a three-year-old who's missed his nap?*

"Do you happen to have an envelope or something I could use to keep this hair in?" Mac asked, breaking through the introspective man's fog.

Silas opened his wallet and took out one of the small evidence bags he always kept with him. *Focus on the procedure!* "I sure hope this gives us a clue about who he is," he said, holding open the plastic envelope so Mac could put the hair in it. "Oh, and just curious, do you have an app on that fancy phone of yours to test this? Or do I have to send it to one of the labs in this time and wait for months or years for an answer?"

34

"Sorry, Silas," Mac said. "I can't do anything with this other than hand it over to you. I seriously doubt it will ID the man but who knows? Maybe he messed up somewhere and he's already in a database. It may not tell us where he is but could let us know where he's been."

Benji looked from Mac to the stranger that got along with him so well and so fast. "Now, tell me, who is this Julianna person…" He saw Silas start to speak with a politician's vagueness and clarified, "Who she is to me and my wife?"

Jane stood up suddenly. "Someone's coming down the road." She moved closer to the edge of the porch and put her hand over her eyebrows and squinted. "I can't see the color of the car because it's kicking up so much dust."

Silas joined her, noticing she was a full four inches taller than he was. He tiptoed and peered out, too. "Inbound fast but unknown vehicle."

Mac stayed seated, eyes closed, concentrating on the sound of the motor. "I'd say it was a small diesel engine, probably a Mercedes or BMW." He chuckled. "Probably the realtor. They like those fancy rigs."

Benji moved to Jane's other side. "We'll see soon," he said, then patted her arm. "Let's wait for him to come to us."

They all returned to their barrel perches, silently waiting, too tense to start – or finish – a topic of conversation.

A portly man with a carefully coifed blond toupee and mirrored sunglasses braked to a fast and dusty stop parallel to the porch. He glanced into his rearview mirror out of habit, verifying his hairpiece was tidy and in place, then stepped out of the BMW roadster without turning off the engine. He'd make this a fast stop.

"What are you doing here?" he asked the group sharply. "You set off all sorts of alarms. This place is under surveillance, you know."

Mac and Benji stood up. Silas considered it, then realized that the two giant men would be much less impressive if a gray-haired six-footer stood beside them. He looked over at Jane. "I think they got this," he whispered.

She looked at him with one eyebrow raised but didn't say a word. *You think?*

He chuckled. She spoke without talking, too.

"Are ye the realtor?" Benji asked.

"Is this your son?" the man replied, looking from one man to the other, then to the very dark-skinned woman seated behind them.

"Who he is wouldna be any concern of yers. Now, I'm askin' ye again, are ye the realtor? I'd say ye must be by name on the side of the car. Larry Lawrence Limited? So, are ye Mr. Lawrence or Mr. Limited?"

Mac and Silas stifled their chuckles while Jane watched the perimeter of the property. The short hairs on her arms were rising and it wasn't the small breeze that had just kicked in. She sniffed discreetly and smelled flowers. Chemical fragrance, not natural. She glanced over at Silas. He was looking at her. He smelled it, too. He leaned forward so she could look behind him into the brush. Four eyes were better than two.

"My name is Larry Lawrence," the indignant man said. "And you are under citizen's arrest for breaking and entering."

"We didn't break in anywhere," Benji said coolly. "Check the lock fer our prints. They aren't ours. Someone was here before us. Ye'd ken that if ye had a proper surveillance system, not jest a tripwire and those phony plastic boxes up there."

The realtor followed Benji's gaze and saw how ridiculous the faux cameras looked. He huffed in resignation. "So, why are you here?"

"Isna this place fer sale?"

"Yes, it is," he said, his scolding attitude now a crow of pride mixed with excitement. The realtor rolled his shoulders, getting himself psyched up to make a sale. "I'm sorry we got off on the wrong foot. So, I understand now that you didn't break into this place. Are you interested?" Did you have a chance to look around?

Benji shook his head. "Before I invest any of my time or money, I have a few questions. Acreage, water, sewer, electricity, gas… What are the stats? Give me the spiel."

"You're from Scotland, aye?" the realtor asked, his tone and demeanor completely cordial now that he had a prospective client in front of him instead of a crook.

"I spent some time there," Benji said. "That doesn't make a difference on whether I buy this place or not, though, does it? Nor does the color of my family?" he asked, eyes narrowed in suspicion.

"Any sale will go through if the money is right. One point five million will get you this lovely plot of two-hundred acres of land on the spring-fed Greek Creek that runs twelve months a year. Yes, there's power here, both single and three-phase. And you have a septic system so you'll never have to pay a sewer bill."

Benji scowled and shook his head. He knew the property values. He'd thought about buying in this area when he was building the house for Bibb Melbourne three years ago. Larry's asking price was inflated by nearly fifty percent. It was time to negotiate.

"Let's see," Benji said. "This site has a few assets with the well and septic, but most of the places around here are set up the same. The house, though." He shook his head and uttered a soft, "Tsk, tsk."

"What? People pay extra to buy land with historical buildings," the realtor argued.

"Aye, if they're in livable condition. This one isna even good enough fer the vermin." He stood back and watched as a mouse ran in front of his boot into the overgrown shrubbery. "I'd say ye needed to drop the price by half considerin' the shape of the house and the lack of a barn."

"Bare land of this size would be at least a million," Larry said, chin out.

"Maybe bare land with a new irrigation system and fields ready to seed."

The realtor's shoulders slumped, wordlessly backing down from that point, agreeing.

"I think seven-hundred-thousand dollars is more than a fair price," Benji said.

"Nine-hundred, fifty-thousand," Larry countered.

Mac had been following the conversation. He'd seen the historical documents from his time and knew the final price. His fists clenched in anticipation.

"Seven-fifty," Benji said and smacked the timber above his head, watching bits of rotted lumber drift to the ground.

"I might be able to do nine if the owner is willing," Larry said.

Mac stood up, startling the realtor. "I've seen the disclosure," he said. "This property is owned by a company you run under your wife's maiden name." He turned to Benji, grinned, then sat back down. "Just saying."

"No, I think nine-hundred thousand is still too much," Benji said.

Now it was Mac's turn for slumped shoulders. That's what the final purchase price for this place had been. Was this sale going to fall through because his grandfather was stingy with a few bucks?

A cell phone rang with a soft buzz-buzz, interrupting the negotiations.

The three time-travelers ignored it, knowing it wasn't theirs. Larry blushed at being the source of disruption, then reached into his pocket and took out his phone. He was ready to push the end button and send it to voice mail when saw the caller ID. His eyes widened. "Excuse me just a moment, please."

He turned from the group to speak. "Yes, yes; tomorrow at noon would be perfect. I'll meet you at the escrow office downtown. Oh, and thank you very much. I'm sure you'll be happy with it." The realtor ended the call and turned back around. "Sorry about that. I've been waiting on him for two months."

Benji shot a glance at Mac. He had seen the young man's body language. He probably knew the final numbers on this transaction. It didn't matter. He wasn't going to change how much he was willing to spend on this place. That would truly be messing with the shape of things to come.

Benji returned his attention to the realtor. "I'd say by the smile on yer face that all went well. So, back to this. I *am* motivated, but I also ken there are at least three other properties in this area that would fit my needs. I'd wager yer not the agent on all of them, though, are ye?"

The realtor shook his head, holding back his elation at the good news of the phone call he'd just received. He could sell this property for six and break even. Anything over that was pure profit. "I'll tell you what, if you're willing to shake hands on this right now, I'll let it go for eight-twenty-five and you pay all the costs."

Benji squinted, seeing the realtor was holding something back. "I'll tell ye what, I'll be willing to pay those as long as the total does not exceed nine-hundred. Every penny over that will be yer responsibility."

"Deal," Larry said, hand stuck out. *I knew I'd find a sucker to pay that seventy-thousand dollar back property tax bill.*

"Larry Lawrence, we have an agreement. If ye'll give me yer information, I'll text ye my phone number. Give me a call when ye have the paperwork together, ready fer our signatures."

"And dollars," the realtor said with a wink, handing him his business card.

As Benji shook hands on the deal, he noticed Silas jerk awake. He'd fallen asleep sitting up and now looked panicked. "Now, if ye have places to go, I think my friends and I will take a walk around the place and see what I got myself and my wife into."

The realtor gladly accepted his dismissal and was back to his air-conditioned car in a flash, ready to write two contracts totaling nearly three million dollars. What a great day!

Benji sat down on the barrel next to Silas. "What's ailin' ye? Ye look like ye jest swallowed a bug."

Silas gave a nervous smile. "If only it was that pleasant. Bad dreams." He sniffed, smelling the scent he'd fallen asleep to. "Do you smell that, too?"

"I do," Jane said. "It smells like flowers."

Benji sniffed, turning his head as he followed the scent carried on the gentle breeze. "It's coming from down there," he said, pointing toward the bushes on the side of the porch opposite the driveway.

Mac jumped over the steps and was where his grandfather had pointed to in a flash. "It smells like lilies of the valley."

"Actually, it's a perfume called Lily of Lourdes," Silas said, now standing behind Mac, sniffing at the trail of scent. "And here's its source." He bent over and picked up a pale pink floral scarf, rolled into a cylinder. "Put your hands out," he told Mac.

Mac gave him a quizzical look but did as told.

"I don't have a worktable," Silas said. "If something's in here, it will fall into your hands, not onto the ground."

"Sounds like you've done fieldwork before," Mac said.

"My nickname's Sherlock. I guess it's considered a hobby since I've never charged for my services," he said as he carefully unwound the fabric.

Benji and Jane joined the duo, standing close enough to see but not to be in the way. "There!" Jane said. "Look, there's something written on it."

"Coins 4 J," Silas read. He folded it in half and shook it over Mac's hands, hoping a scrap of evidence would drop. "There! Grab it before the wind catches it."

Mac held onto one long curly dark-brown hair. "Do you recognize the scarf?" he asked, looking at Silas.

"It's Julianna's. So is the hair, I think."

"Let's put this whole conversation on pause fer a moment," Benji said, looking between Silas and Mac, then back at Jane to make sure she understood his reference. She nodded that she did. "I asked ye before and we were interrupted by Larry and a sales negotiation, so I'm asking ye again: who is this Julianna to me and my wife?"

Silas turned to Mac, asking him with a look, 'Which one of us should answer?' Mac shrugged, so Silas replied. "She's your daughter. And also my fiancée or girlfriend, depending on her answer…when I get a chance to ask her."

"I thought Mali was our daughter," Jane said, her hand gently touching her lower belly.

"They both are," Mac said.

"Julianna's your second born," Silas added. "By the clock, I met her four months ago. By the calendar, it was five years. She came back from 2032 to 1989, looking for Mali. She's never found her as far as I know. I mean, I re-met her at a wedding. We recognized each other from Woodstock in 1969."

"But you just said she went to 1989, not 1969," Benji said.

Jane held her hand up in the air, trying to get their attention.

"Yes?" all three men asked at the same time.

"Can we continue this discussion in the shade. Oh, and start by trying to figure out what the message on the scarf means. As far as I'm concerned, first things first. Keep my daughter safe!"

Chapter 8

The group went back to the porch, Silas holding the scarf with the message folded out reverently, trying to keep his emotions in check at the loss of 'J.' *But she was just here. How could he have snatched her and left a note so quickly? Something doesn't feel right.*

"Does 'Cash 4 J' mean anything to you, Mac?" he finally asked.

"You really need to get some sleep, Silas," Mac replied. "It says coins, not cash. Big difference."

"Especially when it comes to time travelers, aye?" Benji said with a grimace. "I only have the one. I used mine to bring Janie here from the 18th century. I still have it in a safe place. And he's askin' fer coins, not 'a' coin."

Mac held up his wristwatch with his Greek drachma nestled between the crystal and the timepiece mechanism. "My one and only," he said.

Silas groaned softly and shook his head.

"What?" Mac and Benji asked at the same time.

"Julianna and I had one for each of us. She said she had hidden a bag of them here at the MacKay Manse a long time ago. That's why we were coming here – to get them."

"Well, where are they hidden?" Benji asked. "We'll give him those and get her back."

"It's not that easy," Silas said. "Even as ditzy as I'm feeling right now, I don't believe he really has her. I think this is a fake ransom note, meant to make us retrieve the coins for him."

"Maybe they're still here. Where did the girls hang out when they were younger?" Mac asked Jane, then winced in embarrassment. "Shoot! I'm sorry. They haven't even been born yet. You wouldn't know, would you?"

"Well, maybe I would," Jane said with a sly grin. "If I lived here as a child – and I did over two hundred years ago – I'd be out there at the trees, playing in whatever water was available, enjoying the shade."

"Now that's some clever thinking," Silas said. "Shall we walk or drive?"

"If that Storm troublemaker is still around, he'd see us if we drove the truck. Remember how Janie saw that cloud of dust long before Larry

41

showed up in his little sports car? I'd say we space ourselves about ten feet apart and look for a trail or signs left behind by…" Benji paused and mused, rolling the name over in his head before he said it aloud, "Julianna."

"I've never heard that name before," Jane said, "but I like it."

"It reminds me of a dear friend, my Uncle Wallace's stepfather," Benji said. "Julian Hart. Yes, even if ye hadna told me about it, I'd lean toward choosing the name Julianna fer a second daughter."

"Then let's get moving and see what we find at those trees," Silas said. "And if Julianna's there, the second thing I'm going to do is ask her to marry me."

"What's the first thing?" Mac asked.

"Make sure she's all right and not in danger."

Mac walked back to his rental truck and pulled bottles of water out of the back. "Hydrate, everyone. Plus, once we're there, we'll have a container or two to pull a sample from the creek."

Jane looked up at Benji, unsure of what Mac had just said. Benji said softly, "He says to make sure we drink water. He can use the empty bottles to check the purity of the creek."

"Well, why didn't he just say so," she whispered.

"Make sure you're SD10," Mac said to everyone.

"Huh?" they all asked.

"Even I don't know that one," Silas said. "And I just came from a few years ago."

"Sorry. That's Social Distancing ten feet," Mac said. When he noticed they still didn't get it, he clarified. "Social distancing is keeping apart from other people. Standard is six feet away, but just to be sure infectious matter doesn't spread further while outside because of wind conditions, a ten-foot distance is deemed safer."

"Keep away from each other so we don't catch each other's germs?" Silas asked.

"Well, that's the spacing factor and the original reason for it, but this time, it's so we don't kick up as much dust."

"Does that mean there's some horrible disease coming?" Benji asked.

"As I said when we first met," Mac reiterated, "make sure you have a year's supply of food, medicines, and paper products. I can't say when or if it will ever happen, especially since Storm is running around,

42

possibly skewing up the timeline. I don't know if he's in any way responsible for what comes. Just keep plenty of toilet paper on hand in case of a Charmageddon."

"I get that one," Silas said. "A world running-out-of-toilet-paper disaster."

"I would laugh," Benji said, "but I take that it's serious. It's more than running out of personal products, aye?"

"Aye," Mac said, a somber glower on his face, remembering the friends he had lost to the virus. "Spread out and remember to look down. And stay atop weeds or grass if possible so you don't send up a dust signal that we're coming."

Twenty feet from the trees, they all heard it. Giggles from two females coming from up high in the branches, and then a 'shush' admonition. "Someone might hear us," one voice whispered.

"Julianna!" Silas hollered, running to the source, ignoring Mac's warning to be discreet.

Thump!

Julianna dropped out of the trees. "Shush!" she repeated. "He might still be here."

"Who?" Silas whispered.

She looked around to see if he was alone, then saw three people come forward slowly, each one staring at her as if she had a purple horn sticking out of her forehead. "Mom? Dad? And who are you?"

Thump!

Another woman dropped from the branches, also agile despite her forty-something years. "Mac?" she asked. Before he could answer, she whispered, "It is you, isn't it?"

Mac's chest swelled and tightened at the same time as an unexpected explosion of happiness tried to burst through his ribcage. He thought he would always be angry at her for leaving, but there was no rage in him now as he swooped her up in his arms. "Yes, it's me. I grew a bit while you were gone."

Mali held him tight, pulled away briefly to inspect him, then started plastering his cheeks with kisses. "I'm so sorry. So, so sorry. I had to leave or he would have killed you." She pulled back from planting another kiss, her face flushed with terror.

"You shouldn't have come back for me. He's here – in this time. He wants to kill you," she said.

Silas was inspecting Julianna, patting her shoulders, pausing his wellness check to cup her cheeks, and ask, "Are you sure you're all right?"

Benji held Jane close as they watched the couples, stunned. They were seeing their daughters for the first time as adults, completely passing – and missing – their infant through teen years.

"Mom," Mac said, trying his best to reassure her before facing the confusion of introducing his grandparents to their children, "he's already been here. He's gone."

"Then he'll be back," she said. "I've kept him from you all these years," her voice became harsh and scolding, "and then you pop in and mess up everything!"

"Excuse me? I come here looking for the mother who abandoned me, hoping to make things right with her, and you tell me I'm messing things up?"

"Well… Yes," Mali said, then looked at her squealing younger sister.

Silas was down on one knee. "You're sure you wouldn't mind being married to an old man with gray hair?"

She squealed again, and this time, grabbed him by the elbows and pulled him to his feet. "Gray hair, blue hair, or no hair – yes! I want to marry you."

Mali turned her attention back to Mac. "I was trying to lure Storm to the house so he could be arrested. Something must have changed, though. Just like the first time, he ransacked the house looking for the coins, then left to get his tool kit. I was going to alert the authorities when he came back the second time. But instead of *him* showing up, it was you and…"

Mali paused and stared at the couple ten feet away. "Oh, my God! It is them, isn't it?" she asked, suddenly realizing who Mac had brought with him.

"You look so young," she said, walking toward them. "But you *are* young, aren't you?"

A surge of nausea hit Jane as Mali neared. She brought one hand to her mouth, the other to cover her tightening womb.

Benji felt her falter and held on tighter. "Jest a moment," he said, motioning for her to stop. "I'm a bit leery of greetin' ye at this time."

44

Jane took a sip from her water bottle. "I think it was just excitement or morning sickness," she said. "I feel fine now." She reached out and touched the hand Mali still held out.

"Mom, you don't know me," she said. "I love you so much. I made some horrible mistakes. I thought I was an adult, but I was just tall, that's all. I don't know how I can make it up to you and Da, but I'll try. I mean, I can be in two places at once if that's what you're afraid of."

Benji's one eyebrow rose, confirming that was his fear. Mali kept hold of her mother's hand and with the other, reached up and touched her father's temple. "Not even one gray hair. Sorry, I guess I'm the one who gave them to you."

"Ahem," Mac cleared his throat loudly to get everyone's attention. "We're at a crucial point in time right now. It seems that Storm was due to come back here and raise more havoc. It may be that our encounter on the road interrupted his plans. I do know he seemed to recognize me. Either that, or he plays chicken with all vehicles on deserted back roads."

"Hmph," Mali said. "He'd rather win by persuasion or intimidation than with fists or brute force. He can cause more damage that way."

"That's okay, sweetie," Julianna said, now at her sister's side, reassuring her. "None of this was your fault. He was a smooth operator for years before he met you. You just got sucked up into his big plan. I'm sure you having a child wasn't part of it."

"I'm positive about that part. When I told him I thought I was pregnant, he tried to talk me into an abortion. I said, 'I'll see,' and..." Mali looked at the shocked faces of her sister and parents and shook her head, reassuring them. "I said, 'I'll see,' and then lied. I told him all was well. I figured lying was a weak sin compared to killing an unborn child."

A collective sigh came from everyone but Mali. "And so as soon as I found the chance – and before I started showing – I disappeared. He didn't find me until Mac was almost two."

"So, I have to ask," Mac said, "why does he want to kill me? I've never met the man. I wouldn't even know he existed if you hadn't told me about what he said when he saw me in the park that day."

"There's a legend," Mali started, then cleared her dry throat. Mac offered her his water bottle.

"There's always a legend," Benji mumbled as she took a sip.

Mali uttered a soft, 'Grr," accompanied by a scowl.

Benji chuckled. "I have the feelin' this is the first of many times I'll hear and see that reaction."

"Well, yeah. Sorry. Sorta," she said, chuckling. She took a deep breath and started on the somber subject. "The legend is the world will bow to a Red Storm until he is undone by his son."

"Okay…" Mac said. "So, I see how he's the Red Storm, him having red hair and all, but am I the only son?"

"No," Julianna said.

Mali turned to her, shocked. "What? I didn't know he had any others. How many?"

"Only one that I know of," she said.

"Well, why didn't you tell me?" Mali asked.

"You've been a little hard to find the last twenty-two years, big sister," Julianna answered harshly.

"Yeah, well… You could have let me know when you first got here."

"Less than an hour ago? You haven't stopped talking since I found you up in that tree. When was I able to get a word in? Shoot! If everyone here hadn't shown up, you'd still be talking. Just like always. You have to be in charge of everything. You know better than everyone else what's most important."

"Seems like ye were able to get a word in, even if it was edgewise," Benji said, grinning. "I take it the two of ye are always like this."

"We were," Mali said. "I'm sorry. Really, I am. So, Mac might not be the target?"

Julianna shrugged but stayed mute.

"Excuse me," Silas said. "If I may offer an observation. If the legend is true, I would think that this Storm person would try to eradicate all of his progeny, not just Mac. How do you know there is another one, dear?"

"He's my son."

Chapter 9

"You have a child?" Silas asked, his voice ending on a high note of surprise.

"You've met him," Julianna said, eyebrows narrowed. "We were all there at the wedding. Remember Oscar?"

"Um, yes. But he's white..."

Julianna interrupted him, her tone curt with frustration. "And you and everyone else who matters to me knows he's adopted. That's never been a secret."

"I'm aware of that, but is Storm your former husband?" Silas asked, sweat beading on his upper lip. He tried to wipe it away without showing how distraught he was, then realized no one here would judge him and finished the gesture without shame.

"No. My husband couldn't have children," she replied, her tone and attitude normal now that she saw he wasn't being judgmental. How could he forget about Oscar, his granddaughter's boyfriend?

"Then how did you wind up with Storm's baby?" he asked.

"Well, you met my adopted brother, Rick Rickman, at the wedding, right?"

"Yes, briefly. I heard no matter what your issues, he stood by you. You were his favorite sister."

"I was his only sister. His parents adopted me when I was sixteen. I had been living at the shelter his family supported, bussing tables at a local café to make a few bucks. His mother saw me in front of work one day. My boss had just fired me for breaking a cup and I was having a meltdown. She put her arm around my shoulder and said, 'You're coming home with me.' They had just moved to England from America and Rick was eleven at the time. He loved that he finally had a big sister. 'The bigger the better,' he used to say."

"Why were ye staying at a shelter?" Benji asked. "Why dinna ye come home to us? Were we that horrible?"

"No! It wasn't you I was running away from at all. I didn't want to come home without Mali. Plus, I couldn't. I didn't have a drachma – or at least the right one. Did you know that a gold one won't work? Anyhow, I'd followed Mali to 1969 Woodstock – which is where I met

Silas the first time. After that, I wound up getting a job on a cruise ship and made my way to London."

Julianna paused her story and frowned at Silas in a playful manner. "Mali and I were just catching up with where we've been and such when you sneaked up and almost scared us out of the trees."

"Sorry about that," Silas said with a broad smile, happy to have her back. "Proceed."

"I wanted to slip forward to 1989 which is *when* I figured she would be. You see," she looked at Mali who was listening silently, keeping a wary eye on the house. She returned Julianna's glance, grinned weakly, then turned back to her sentry task. "You see, I figured Mali wanted to stop the oil spill in Valdez, Alaska that year. I was hoping to get there by working on another cruise ship. My coin had been stolen, though. So, even if I could be in the right place, I wouldn't be able to go back. I was stuck." She chuckled and shook her head in disbelief. "Yeah, stuck with a very rich and loving family, and a little brother who thought I was the queen of the world."

Silas cleared his throat. "Sorry to interrupt, but could we skip forward to the baby part?"

"Years later, I married a man and he and I adopted the baby – Storm's baby. A little backstory, though. I now ran the shelter where I used to live. A new homeless woman showed up one day. Everyone thought Ciara was crazy. She was obsessive about handwashing, asking everyone she met if they had been immunized, always insisting on maintaining social distancing. No one had heard of that term, though. They chalked it up to schizophrenia. She wasn't crazy, though. She was a time traveler. I called her aside and made a comment that put her at ease."

"What did you say?" Silas asked.

"I told her it was 1989. COVID hadn't hit yet," Julianna said. "That was enough to stop her paranoia and also let her know I was from the future, too. She was very pregnant and very scared. Some of the others at the shelter wanted her kicked out or put in a mental hospital. I told them she was harmless, couldn't live on the streets, and the hospital might make her take medications that would affect her unborn baby. 'Besides,' I said, 'just because she had a stalker and was cautious about infections didn't mean she was nuts.' That shut them up.

"Just having someone to talk to – and who understood why she was so afraid – calmed Ciara enough that she started to fit in. She made me promise that if anything happened to her, I'd take care of her baby."

"So, something happened to her in childbirth?" Silas asked.

"No. She just left. Or someone took her. I'm not sure. I helped the midwife deliver her of a healthy boy. I brought her back to the shelter and visited her every day. I missed the fourth day, and by the fifth, she was gone. Just gone. One of the other directors, Hugh, was taking care of Oscar when I came back. I think I was in shock. There I was with a baby and a promise. He said he wanted to help but it was more than that.

"He knew Ciara had asked me to take care of her child if something happened to her, so he suggested we get married. We could adopt Oscar together. He wanted to make it legal. Plus, he was pretty fond of me. We had worked together for years. He told me later that he'd wanted to ask me out on a date for ages but didn't know how to.

"I could have gone back home with the Rickman's and brought up Oscar by myself, but Hugh had already bonded with him. So, we married. He got the woman he wanted and the heir he craved. Oscar was everything to him.

"But I had a dilemma. I still had to find the right silver drachmas, so when I found Mali, I could bring her home. But I couldn't go traipsing across the world or time with a baby, and there's no way I was going to leave Oscar behind. So, I figured I'd wait until he was a little older. Well, time flew by. My life was full with an attentive husband and a charming son. I put my search on hold until he started school. I never found the coins but didn't stop looking for them or an alternate means of time travel.

"Hugh didn't like that I was spending so much time and money on researching it. He remembered I had told him Ciara – Oscar's birth mother – was a time traveler. He had thought I was a bubble off center back then but now was sure of it. When I wouldn't go to psychiatrists voluntarily, he pulled some strings and had me committed. The doctors put me on antipsychotic drugs. I had an adverse reaction to them..." Julianna said, rolling her eyes to finish her revelation without giving her parents any humiliating details.

"So, how did you know about the legend?" Silas asked, hoping to get her back on topic.

Julianna snorted a quick laugh. "When I first met Ciara and mentioned 'COVID,' she paled. She said her old boyfriend – the father of her unborn child – was behind it. She had tried to sneak his stash from him and destroy it, but he caught her. 'Storm's temper was redder than his hair,' she told me. That led to us comparing notes about her Storm and the man Mali had been seeing after basketball practice. I knew a little about him: his name, that he was as tall as Da, and his hair was just as bright red. He was white but didn't have freckles. I had never seen him, though."

"His stash of what?" Benji asked, perplexed.

"He had stolen a virus from a lab – very contagious and deadly. All he'd have to do is spritz a few shots in strategic airports, and it'd spread worldwide in days." Mali looked at Julianna. "As far as being immunized against it, you and I are the only ones…" she paused and saw Mac scowling at her. "Sorry. I forgot about you," she said.

"Again," Mac huffed.

"No! Not again. Not really. I mean, excuse me if I have a hard time associating this tall, handsome man with the little curly-haired boy who loved to play hide and seek. I guess I should have known you'd get so tall, but in my mind, you're still a ten-year-old."

Kaboom!

All eyes went toward the house. Or where the house had been. It was now a six-story high dust cloud sprinkled with timbers and roof tiles, swirling in place like a tan tornado.

"What in the…" Silas asked.

"And there it goes," Mac said dryly, shaking his head.

"What? Ye ken that was going to happen?" Benji barked, his fists clenched in rage.

"Yeah, well, eventually," Mac replied, not in the least bit intimidated. "I didn't know whether it would be today or next month. I only knew it would be after you agreed to buy the place but before you moved in." He saw the frustration on his young grandfather's face. "Hey! If I thought we were in danger, I would have spoken up! I did know no one was going to die or be injured in it." Mac thumped his chest, then nodded to Mali. "Mom and I wouldn't be here if that was the case."

"Aye, yer right there," Benji admitted. "On the plus side, I guess I jest saved a few thousand dollars in demolition costs."

"Huh?" Jane asked.

"I don't have to rent a bulldozer or pay anyone to knock it down for me. I will have to get some equipment in here to clean up the mess, though." Benji stepped aside and watched the dust settle, searching. "There's no fire, is there?"

"Nope," Mac said. "That was a mystery then, too. They never figured out what happened. There was no power turned on, so it couldn't have been caused by an electrical short. Spontaneous methane gas build-up was speculated, but there wasn't a fire."

"If you'll allow me," Silas said. He brought out his smartphone, swiped and tapped. "Ah... Nope. Nobody. Nothing. No one came or went while we were gone. I'd say Red Storm planted a bomb or two when he was here earlier. And the wind is blowing the right way so Mac's rental vehicle is safe."

Mac and Benji came over to see what he was doing. "What do ye have there?" Benji asked, looking over Silas as Mac leaned over the other shoulder.

Silas blinked back his discomfort at being crowded by two concerned giants and pointed to the phone's screen. He swiped the timeline at the bottom of the image and backed up the video. "I stuck a camera on the back of the rearview mirror of the truck. I'd say we have someone who's an expert in demolition. Looks like a clean implosion."

"If it has to do with destruction," Mali said, "Storm's your man."

"Can you tell us more?" Silas asked her.

"When I left with him, I thought he just wanted to bounce through time to watch cataclysmic events. I was so wrong. He wanted to cause them. We need to stop him."

Silas held up the pink scarf with the note written on it. "So, what does 'Coins for J' mean?"

"Well, um... I may have told him that my dad had a big bag of time travel coins at the house. The new house, not the old one," Mali said with a grimace of guilt. "I guess he was just here to make sure a new one was built."

Chapter 10

"So, what now?" Mali asked.

Benji took his phone and Larry's business card out of his pocket. "I think I owe the realtor some contact information. Not that the house imploding is any concern of his since we already shook hands on the deal."

"But Da…" Mali whined, ready to argue about what needed to be done first.

He fixed her in place with a squint of confusion blended with admonishment. "Do ye ken how disconcerting it is to have a woman I've never seen and who seems to be my elder call me Da? And, whether ye really are my daughter or not, ye'll ken that this is my property and what happens on it is my business."

"Yes, sir," Mali replied somberly, her pre-teen submissive attitude returned with his gentle scolding.

"But what should we do about this?" Silas asked, holding up the scarf with the impromptu extortion message on it.

Benji grinned. "Give it back to yer fiancée. I'd invite ye to stay fer dinner, but it looks like both our kitchen and dining room are out of service. Mac, if ye dinna mind, after I send this text to Mr. Lawrence, would ye join Jane and me on a walk around the perimeter?"

"To see what you got yourself into?" Mac asked with a grin of devilment.

Benji answered with an intriguing grumble of mischief, then snorted in resignation and said, "Oh, who knows? There may be other points of interest around here. Or maybe a few more of my progeny will drop out of the trees."

Mac groaned at the joke, making sure he didn't let on how close to the truth it was. "Ach! Do what you need to, Grandpa, so we can get on with it. It may be nearing autumn, but it's still hot and muggy by noon. I'd prefer to finish my walking before then." *Don't let him know how many children he winds up with or you'll scare him witless.*

Benji looked down and texted his information, then put the phone away. "Tell me," he said to Mac, "how much do ye ken about what happens next? Is something else destined to blow up while I stand by and watch?"

"I couldn't say."

"Couldn't or won't?" Benji asked, one eyebrow raised.

"Won't. Shouldn't. Does it matter?" Mac answered. "You just proved when you were negotiating the price of this place that you were going to spend what you wanted, not what I knew it to be, right?"

"Aye, there's that. I learned long ago that no matter how much ye try to avoid a situation, if it was meant to be, it will happen. The price was the same in the end, right?"

Mac nodded, then looked over at Jane. She was sipping on a bottle of water, watching her two middle-aged daughters bickering with each other. So much like her in looks but not in demeanor. "Even if you have to go back in time over two hundred years to find true love, right?" Mac asked Benji.

"I'd do it all over again. Maybe one of these days, we'll have time enough to share the stories of our first week together. A relationship that shouldn't have been..." Benji sighed, then fixed Mac with a hard look. "Never take lightly that true love only comes once in a lifetime."

"Well, I've never even sniffed at it, much less seen it up close," Mac said.

"I recall a time when I got frustrated because I was in the same situation. Who knows? If yer from the future, maybe the lass fer ye is in this time."

"I'm not looking," Mac said.

"Nor was I," Benji replied, his hand patting him on the shoulder. "Jest treat every woman with respect, no matter what her station in life."

"Even if she's a slave..."

"Even if she's a slave valued at less than two dollars," Benji said and looked lovingly at Jane.

"Are we ready?" she asked, glancing up toward the sun that was rising, sending the heat index higher, then back at him.

"Let's go," Benji agreed.

The men and Jane headed off, leaving the two women and Silas at the truck. "Wait!" Silas called out. "I'm going with you if you don't mind."

"Too much girl chatter?" Mac asked.

"Girl chatter? Oh, yes. I guess they've always been this way. Julianna said they've been argumentative with each other since day one, but nobody had better bad mouth the other when they were around! Right

53

now, they're trying to figure out which time they should stay in." Silas rolled his eyes. "As if it makes a difference."

The four walked single file, following a thin trail toward the fence line. "It looks like a dog's been patrolling the perimeter," Silas said, his words bringing them all to a halt.

Benji turned around and asked, "And how do ye figure that?"

Silas held up a tuft of fur. "Big dog by the height of where I found this. The ground's too covered with dead grass and weeds to see the size of his paw prints. He or she's been following the same trail for quite a while, though. By the break in the blades, I'd say he was through here early this morning."

"He's either a neighbor's critter or verra fond of the place," Benji said.

"Or he was left behind to fend for himself," Jane said coolly.

Both men looked at her and saw the same bitter scowl.

"Sounds like ye ken of a few animals like that."

"One was too many. I don't want to talk about it," she said, then straightened her back and looked at the horizon, trying to forget her past as an 18th-century slave.

"If we find the pup and he doesn't have a place to stay, we'll build him a porch, all right?" Benji said, his hand on her back.

Jane turned around sharply. "What if he's an old dog, though?" she asked, ready to stand up for the unknown and unseen critter.

"Then I'll build him a bed. In the winter, he can lay inside at the hearth."

"A pet. A summertime porch dog," Jane said, her eyes shining as she recalled one of her most hoped for wishes as a child. "Let's keep moving. I think I can tell you about him if we're walking."

The four began again. "Duke was a white dog with black spots. I guess the master used him for hunting. Anyhow, he became lame when he stepped in a trap."

"Ouch," Benji said.

"The master had told his son to shoot him. The boy was only ten or so at the time. He was a gentle soul and had never taken to hunting. The master wanted to toughen him up – make a man out of him. The other kids and I rescued the hound by making a deal with the son. He could shoot the gun into a bush, then we'd smear chicken blood around so it looked like he'd killed the dog. He could tell his pa the body was gone because he told us to bury it."

"The old man bought it for a day or two, then found out ye had him…" Benji suggested.

"That gimpy dog was only ours for a week, but having a pet was a rare treat." Jane looked up, glad he had spared her telling the end of the story. Saying the words out loud was a lot harder than just thinking about them. "I think I see the fence," she said, ending her sad memory by changing focus.

A few long strides and they were there. "More than a fence," Silas said. "I think this part is a survey marker." He took a pair of reading glasses out of his pocket and looked closer at the spray-painted area near the top of the post. Then he noticed the upright was cemented into the ground, not just stuck in the soil. The little concrete platform had a brass marker embedded in it with the same letters and numbers stamped into it. "Yup. This is a landmark and these are the legal coordinates." He took out his phone and snapped a picture. "Just in case the numbers on your deed don't match up with these."

"Now I know why they call you Sherlock," Mac said. "Thanks. You just saved me from dropping another hint."

"Ye ken the realtor would try to keep part of my property from me?"

"Now you know it, too," Mac said. "And just for the record, I never met Silas until you did. I doubt he was here the first time, and I know I wasn't. If he hadn't seen it, either you or Granny would have."

"Why do ye call us that: Granny and Grandpa."

Mac grinned wide enough for his molars to show. "Well, other than the fact that you are, it feels good saying those names. I never had any relatives. I had classmates and friends at school, so wasn't lonely. I know I didn't miss anything by not being around Storm, but it's kind of fun having a grandpa. Besides, I'll bet you can still play a mean game of basketball."

"My second-favorite form of recreation," Benji said with a wink. He swallowed his grin and added, "One of the first things I'll set up after we sign the papers is a half-court."

"Only half?" Mac whined good-naturedly.

"I said that would be *one* of the first. When I'm done with the house and barn, I'll set up a full-court. I'll pass on the bleachers, though. I doubt my family will grow to more than a full team of five plus maybe an alternate."

Mac started to laugh, then realized he was unconsciously negating the remark, so he changed his chuckle into a fake sneeze. "Hayfever," he said as an excuse, knowing that between blood kin and foster children, the MacKays would have more than enough players for two teams.

Benji called the bluff and coughed, "Bullshit," into his hand, then looked at Jane to see if she had heard him. She probably had but wasn't showing it. She was content with where she was as long as they were all together. And he felt the same way.

"Back toward the trees?" Silas asked.

"Yer enjoying this as much as I am, Silas," Benji said. "Who are ye, other than the man with gray hair who's about to be my son-in-law to my yet-to-be-conceived daughter?"

Silas chuckled and stepped aside so Mac could lead the way. "I'm a gentleman's gentleman who inherited a lot of money and property once upon a time. I enjoy fine wine, tall women, witty conversation, and walks through the weeds, getting to know strangers who will soon become kin."

"Sounds like a Playmate biography," Benji said.

"What's a Playmate," Mac asked, noticing that Jane looked confused, too.

"Nothing we need to be concerned with," Benji said, rolling his eyes which Mac understood as, 'I'll tell you later.'

Grrr! Wuff! Wuff!

"Whoa!" Mac exclaimed, hands up in surrender as he took two slow steps backward, nearly bumping into Jane as he moved away from the huge canine guardian.

Jane stepped around Mac and squatted to the ground, her knuckles out. "Why, hello," she said softly. "We're just on a stroll. Sorry to have disturbed you. Are you all right?"

The large motley dog's upper lip relaxed and the growl disappeared as he took hesitant steps toward her. Jane slowly took the water bottle out of her bag and poured a little into her hand. "Are you thirsty?"

The dog lapped it up, then turned around and took a couple of steps back in the direction it had come from. He stopped and looked back over his shoulder, entreating her to follow. "Come on, gentlemen," Jane said. "I think we have a guide wanting to show us something."

Chapter 11

"Do you think he's hurt?" Mac called out to Jane as she followed the dog.

"He didn't say," she replied over her shoulder.

Mac chuckled. "I always heard you had a very dry sense of humor," he said, then added, "Granny."

Benji watched as Jane's shoulders tensed at the title, then relaxed, accepting her new name.

Yip! Yip! Yip! The big spotted dog suddenly bolted, whining a high-pitched bark as he sped down the narrow path. Jane sprinted after him. His call of distress stopped and became a whimper, then resumed, now coming from one spot. Jane made a shortcut through the field, pushing aside the waist-high dry vegetation with her hands and forearms. She ignored the cuts from the razor-edged growth, swimming through the ocean of golden grasses and wild wheat to get to the howling, hysterical dog.

The men rushed to keep up with her on the trail she had blazed, but she stopped them with the shout of, "Stay back!"

And then she was gone, swallowed up by the dried vegetation.

She followed the mutt to a rough nest of matted down groundcover. With him was a young woman laying on her side, barely alive. "You need water," Jane said, offering her the bottle from her daypack.

The semi-conscious female roused. Her hands flew up, pale palms fluttering in front of her dark face, terrorized, trying to fend off an unseen enemy.

"It's just water," Jane said. She held up the bottle, then tipped her head back and dribbled a few drops into her own mouth.

The woman shook her head. Still terrified, the adrenaline coursing through her body had sparked her back to life.

"Are ye okay?" Benji called out.

Jane stood up quickly. "Yes, but hush!" she said, then kneeled next to the woman. "It's all right. That was my husband." Noticing the trail of fresh lash wounds on the woman's bare shoulders, Jane added, "No one here is going to hurt you."

The woman looked down at Jane's bloody arms. "That's just from the grass, coming to find you," she explained. "Here, let me help."

Jane put her hand behind the woman's neck and gently brought her to a seated position. "Head back," she said, glad that the confused and frightened woman understood her. "Open your mouth…" She dribbled a few drops onto her swollen tongue, waited a few seconds, then gave her more.

The woman's eyes blinked as she focused on the bottle that had made strange crackling noises when held. She leaned forward, now able to sit upright by herself, eyes still on the container. She glanced at Jane and, not sensing a threat, reached out to touch the soft glass-like vessel. "More?" she asked, dry voice squeaking.

"Just a sip," Jane said, retaining control of the bottle. She knew it was tempting to guzzle fluids after being dehydrated but remembered that it was best to drink slowly or risk throwing up. She'd been in this same condition many times in her life.

"Here." Jane pulled a colorful bandana out of her daypack and poured water onto it. "Use this."

The woman immediately put it to her mouth and started sucking on it.

"That's not what I meant," Jane said, taking it back, ready to show her how to pat her face and neck with it.

Afraid again, the woman dropped the cloth as if she'd grabbed the wrong end of a branding iron and scooted away, backing into the dry weeds.

"Here," Jane repeated, but this time reached forward and dabbed it on the woman's grimy and dusty face. "You can keep it," she said, making sure the woman would accept the gift. "Are you alone?"

"Dog."

"The dog is the only one here with you?"

She nodded. "Boss Man chased me through the trees after I find this." She held one hand open, showing Jane the silver drachma.

Now Jane was the one with the wide eyes. "Where did you get that?" she asked.

The young woman coughed and nodded to the bottle, asking without words if she could have more.

"Just a little," Jane said.

After a self-regulated short drink, the woman said, "I found it in the dirt. I was going back to give it to Master Joe, but Boss Man saw me first. He yelled at me for not working and came after me with the whip. I just ran and ran and then I was here. The trees look the same but bigger now, but...but the mill is gone. And so is all the people."

Jane emitted an unintentional groan, startling the woman. "I don't know how to tell you," she began.

Before she could find a way to explain, she heard Benji's voice call to her. "Janie, yer scarin' me."

Jane stood up and waved at him, then held her hand open for him to stop coming toward her. "Stay put," she ordered. "She's hurt and disoriented. Give us a minute, then we'll be out."

Squatting back down, she noticed the woman's attire. Or lack of it. In this time, it would be unheard of for a female to be bare-breasted in public. This woman may have come from nearby but wasn't from 'recent.' She had no shame, just fear and thirst. In that order.

"Do you understand tomorrow?" Jane asked.

The woman nodded.

"Do you understand many?"

She nodded again.

"You are many tomorrows away from where you came from."

Jane didn't think it was possible, but the woman's large coffee-brown eyes got wider.

Jane pulled up the back of her shirt and turned away from the woman, showing her the scars on her own back. "I came from many yesterdays, too. I don't know how many for you, but we're safe here. You can have food, and a husband, and even keep your babies where we are now. And no whips. Will you stay with me, with me and my husband?"

The woman looked at the grass lair she'd been living in for two days, too afraid of the barbed wire on the fences and the unknown to go back and see if the creek was still there. She leaned forward, ready to stand up. "Today is many tomorrows?" she asked, making sure she understood.

"Yes," Jane replied. "And no masters or boss men or whips."

"Then I stay with you. I'm Daisy, like the flower."

"And I'm Jane. Glad to meet you." Jane started to help her up, then realized that although Daisy's nakedness didn't bother either one of them, it might make the men uncomfortable.

"Just a minute," Jane said. "I think I have something…" She opened her daypack and brought out her spare bandana. "Let me have that one, please. It's still yours…"

Daisy handed it to her reluctantly, eyebrows crowded as she tried to figure out what the very tall black woman was trying to do.

Jane knotted the two large bandana-style scarves together at two corners, then slipped it over Daisy's head. "All right. Let's stand up," she said, helping her. "Now, let me tie these on the sides." Jane quickly made a loose-fitting blouse with four knots. "We'll get you more clothes later. For now…"

Jane stopped when she saw the smile on Daisy's face. Her full bottom lip was cracked from thirst. Her eyes, once dull from dehydration, were shining with hope and a question waiting to be asked.

"Do you want to tell me something?" Jane asked.

"It's a good tomorrow," Daisy said, giving her the coin. "A mighty fine many tomorrows."

***

Holding Daisy's trembling hand, Jane forged the way through the weeds to the fence line and the clear-cut trail – the easy path back to the men.

When they appeared, no one said a word until Mac stepped forward. "Hi," he said, eyes dancing with enchantment at the ebony woman dressed in paisley kerchiefs and a homespun skirt. "I'm…I'm Mac."

Shocked by his deep baritone voice, Daisy glanced up. When she saw he was grinning at her, a faint smile rose on her own lips before she squelched it in conditioned response and stared at the ground.

She felt Jane's hand squeeze hers in reassurance and looked up again as the introductions began. "So, as he said, this is Mac, and this is my husband, Benji. This gentleman here is our friend, Silas. Men, let me introduce you to Daisy. She, um…" Jane suddenly felt a twinge, remembering her old insecurities about her slave position in life and sniffed it back, looking to Benji, the honorable man who kept telling her she was his equal. "And as long as it's all right with my husband, Daisy will be staying with us."

Benji's eyes widened in surprise and pride. *Her first independent declaration, even if she's giving me the option of negating it!* "Yes, yes. The more the merrier, as they say." He looked at Mac and winked. "Ye dinna see this one comin', did ye?"

Mac was now grinning, ear-to-ear. "If I had, I would have been here sooner."

"If you had," Jane said, "and you were the one who had found her, you might have scared her to death." She looked back at Daisy and saw the humbled woman who – until a couple of days before – had been a slave. She was studying Mac out of the corner of her eye, a talent she had used when she first met Benji a year ago, a time 'many, many yesterdays' past. Yes, it looked like Daisy was as attracted to Mac and he was to her.

Benji watched the silent assessment that Mac, Daisy, and Jane were busy with. "How many people did ye say would be in my family?"

Mac shrugged and returned his gaze to Daisy. "I didn't, and you know that."

What is it about her? Why is she so different than any other woman I've ever met? Why do I want her? Not to possess her as a person, but to have her as part of my world. To create a life together with her. Mac took a deep breath, trying for composure. He exhaled in defeat. He would never be the same callous, hard-shelled man, shunning tenderness and relationships. He was mesmerized by her. Fascinated. Craving her.

He looked up and asked Benji, "So, what was it you called a relationship that shouldn't have been, that once in a lifetime event?" When Mac saw him start to reply with the two words, 'true love,' he stopped him. "That was a rhetorical question. We both know the answer. Grandpa."

"Excuse me," Silas said, "but where is the dog?"

As if on cue, the large spotted mutt 'woofed,' stepping out from behind Daisy.

"Looks like you have one more to add to your family," Silas said. "Is this Duke the Second?"

Benji squatted beside the long-haired Australian shepherd mix and peered underneath, taking a look at the tail-end to verify. "I think she's more of a Duchess. Aye, she's fine to join the twenty-first century MacKay clan."

Jane sighed her appreciation. A pet of her own. Even if she was sharing the dog with others, they were *her* family. *Her* clan. *Their* pet.

"If you want to keep looking at the property, that's fine," Jane told the men, "but I think I need to take Daisy back to the truck and make use of the little bit of shade we have."

"I'll go with you," Mac volunteered, stepping forward eagerly.

Benji noticed Silas wavering from heat, fatigue, or both. "I think we should all return. We've had enough excitement fer today. Plus, this old man needs some sleep," he said, winking at Silas.

"I'd say, 'Speak for yourself,' but in this case," Silas said, "I'll leave pride in the dumpster and grab a nap in the backseat. That is if my darling fiancée remembered where she stashed the car."

Benji led the way, the women and dog behind him, then Silas. Mac brought up the rear, taking the caboose position in case someone faltered.

When they arrived, Silas's vintage pale yellow Cadillac was parked next to Mac's rental truck, doors open. Mali watched them approach from the front seat, Julianna curled up on the back seat, asleep.

Mali stepped out of the car wordlessly and stood beside it, not even trying to hide her suspicious nature. Arms crossed, she tipped her chin up and pointed to the new person in the group. "Who's she?"

"Yer new sister," Benji answered in a no-nonsense voice. *Her status in the family is not open for discussion.*

"Hmph!" Mali replied, uncrossing her arms, placing her hands on her hips. *You don't know anything about her. She just shows up and you bring her in?*

"Move aside so she can sit down," Benji said looking down at her, now nose-to-nose with the woman who had to be his daughter. She certainly had her mother's stubbornness as well as her looks. *I'm still yer father whether I'm twenty years older or younger than ye.*

Mali moved aside and let Jane assist the terrified, scrawny stranger into the passenger seat. "Who is she?" she asked again.

"Her name is Daisy," Jane answered. "And you be nice," she added, then realized her tone was just a sliver from harsh. *I have a Mommy voice?*

"All right, so her name is Daisy," Mali said, "but *who* is she? She doesn't look like she's from around here."

"She is. She came from across the creek," Jane said, still holding Daisy's hand. She changed her focus from Mali to the frightened woman. "Don't mind her," she said. "She'll warm up to you, I'm sure."

"She'd better," Mac said, then added, "right, Mom?"

Mali grunted in defeat at being called out on her rudeness by her adult son. "I still want to know *who* she is, though. There's a lot of serious shit going on."

"Watch yer mouth, young woman," Benji scolded. He took a deep breath as he realized what he had just said and how. "I guess being a parent comes naturally."

"Or some things never change," Mali said sarcastically.

"Have ye always been this sassy?" Benji asked.

"Yes," Julianna answered, awakened from her nap by the familiar bickering. "She'd argue whether water was wet or not just to be contentious."

"It's not wet if it's frozen," Mali replied.

"See?" Julianna said.

Daisy's eyes followed the conversation back and forth between the black women and the white men, shocked at the brazenness of the dark females, confused by some of their unfamiliar words.

Jane saw the fear and patted Daisy's hand. "Ignore them," she said. "They're family. These are my daughters, Julianna and Mali."

"Daughters?" Daisy asked, making sure she had heard correctly. *But they're older than you!*

Understanding 'the look,' Jane addressed it. "They came from many tomorrows."

"Tomorrows?" Daisy asked.

"Yes, just like you came from many yesterdays to today, they came here from many tomorrows. Does that make sense?"

Daisy looked from each of the women to Jane and Benji, and then to Mac. The handsome man with curly red hair was similar in stature to the white man - and much paler than either of the women - but he could be related. He was still smiling at her, a glimmer in his eye that she had seen in men before. She shrank back and looked into her lap, not wanting to engage with anyone with pale skin, even if he had slave heritage.

"Oh, and I'm from many tomorrows, too," Mac said. "This one is my mother. The other one is my aunt. I never met her until today, though. And I only met my grandparents yesterday."

Head still bowed, Daisy gave a furtive glance around, trying to fix relationships in her head.

"Oh, and I'm not related to anyone," Silas said, "but Julianna – the daughter and aunt – and I are engaged to be married. Do you have any questions? I know it's confusing, but we'd like to help you."

"Help me? Why?" she asked so softly, it was more of a whisper.

Mac opened a bottle of water and handed it to her. "Because you look like you need it." He pointed to the oozing scabs on her shoulders. "Someone should look at those wounds. You don't want them to get infected."

"Festered, fevered," Jane said quickly, offering Daisy the traditional words. "We can take care of those problems now."

"So, she's a time traveler from the past?" Julianna asked. "How'd she get here?"

Jane opened her hand and showed her the coin Daisy had given her. Mali reached for it, but Jane tightened her grip and pulled it back. "It's the right one if that's what you're wondering. Drilled, too. And before you start asking questions, she found it on the ground. She was running from the boss man with the whip and wound up here. If I didn't know better – and I don't – I'd say those trees are a portal."

"And running away, visualizing safety from him and no slavery, brought her here," Mac suggested.

"Sounds reasonable," Benji added.

"And now the question is," Silas said watching Daisy's face, "whether it was only one coin or a bag of them she found."

Daisy's eyes widened in surprise, then blinked, bringing back her fear. Had she just traded the hell she knew for one she didn't?

Chapter 12

"Should I start the car and turn on the air conditioning for her?" Julianna asked Silas.

Benji and Jane shouted, "No!"

The couple's sudden loud outburst startled Daisy, and she curled into a ball, knees to her face.

Jane knelt beside her and patted her leg softly. "I'm sorry. You didn't do anything wrong." Then she stood up and looked to Julianna. "I don't know when she's from, but I'll bet she's never heard a car motor. I remember how much it scared me. I thought it was going to explode! We have to take this slow."

"How can we find out when she's from?" Mali asked. "Never mind. I guess it doesn't make a difference."

"I think it does," Julianna said, unintentionally starting another conflict with her older sister. Mali opened her mouth to argue but heard their father clear his voice in a familiar way. She smiled sheepishly as she realized how young he was, then noticed he looked surprised by his automatic parenting response.

"Just think about it," Julianna continued, smirking at Mali with getting a subtle 'proceed' from Da. "If you were dropped into another time, wouldn't you want others to speak with familiar phrases and let you know what is and isn't socially acceptable? What if the word flub meant something rude or waving was obscene?"

Mali snorted as she realized what Julianna meant. She looked at Mac, now all grown up. "When was the last time you touched your mouth without wearing gloves or blew your nose in public?"

"You taught me not to," Mac said, "so never. I've seen a lot of folks doing both here in this time and it gives me the weezies."

"What are the weezies?" Benji asked.

"Pretty much what Julianna's talking about: era-specific slang. It's similar to giving you the creeps," Mali said.

Silas made use of the break in the conversation and waved his hand in the air. "This isn't an obscene gesture anywhere or in any time that I know of, but I want to ask Mac a question. Do you have an app on that phone of yours that can do carbon dating? That little skirt Daisy's wearing looks like homespun cotton. Just a tiny bit of thread ought to be enough."

"You really believe this little device can do that?" Mac asked with an impish smirk on his face. He swiped and pinched the screen on his paperback book-sized device, tapped once, and a tiny piece of dark metal popped out of the side. "Granny, if you would do the honors. Just a half-inch length of thread ought to be enough. She doesn't seem to have much to spare."

Silas brought out his Leatherman multitool, pulled out the tiny scissors, and offered it to Jane. "Here, I think this will help keep rips or tears to a minimum."

Daisy, still seated in the front seat of the Cadillac, watched the men and women chatter back and forth, only understanding about half of what they said. *There's no master or slave between them. Skin color doesn't make a difference. Yes, the two women who are the same age – Julianna and Molly? – behave like sisters. Jane and her husband get along better than any two people of different races that I've ever seen. And they're married! A black woman and a white man!*

A smile came to Daisy's face. *Jane said it was different here. She came from many yesterdays, too. She found a good home in this today. She has nice clothes, a husband, and even this fancy porch with leather seats to sit on.* She touched the custard-colored, soft leather seat in the Cadillac and looked up at Mac. He was stealing glances at her. Still. But she didn't feel threatened or scared. Yes, she was glad she was here. No way would she go back.

"Excuse me," Jane said, breaking into Daisy's musings. "I need to take a little piece of your clothes."

Daisy reached up to remove the knot from her impromptu handkerchief blouse.

"No, no. You can keep that. I just need a wee bit of..." Jane touched the frayed edge of the skirt that only went to mid-thigh. Not even a hem on it. It was simply a rat-chewed flour sack that had been repurposed, a piece of twine woven into the top as a drawstring to keep it around her slim waist. She took a quick snip and gently touched Daisy's cheek. "Thank you. That's all I need."

Daisy grinned meekly, then leaned back into the seat and shut her eyes. *I'm so sleepy. As weak and tired as I've ever been. An hour ago, I was waiting to die. Hoping I'd die.* She opened one eye and peeked at the men and women crowded around Mac, looking at the small closed book he held in his hand. She shut her eyes again. *I want to live now. Tomorrow morning will be better. Much better. I'm sure it will.*

And then she was asleep.

***

"The year of our Lord 1862," Mac said dramatically. "Since it looks like the fabric is at least a year or two old, I'd say she came from 1864."

"Are ye sure?" Benji asked, then realized it was just for argument's sake. *So, I'm who they get the bickerin' gene from!*

"If it was 1865, she would have been emancipated and not a slave. Plus, she's about as thin as a poor excuse. At the end of the war, food was scarce. Slaves ate last. I know she's had water, but I think we ought to get some food in her, too. And we need to make sure it's something her body will recognize. No granola bars or fast food."

"Rice," Jane said. "You're right, though. She needs to eat. I guess it's time for her to come the rest of the way into the twenty-first century."

"At least she's napping in style," Benji said, looking over to the car she now dozed in. "A Cadillac."

"Where to next?" Silas asked. "I'd say we could crash at my place, but that's a few days away in Massachusetts. And wherever it is, I hope Julianna is up to driving. I'm spent."

Benji looked around. He and Jane had rented the motel room so they could look at properties in the area. They were only fifty miles from their temporary home with Bibb and Marty Melbourne. Yes, his favorite elderly couple wouldn't mind having guests. They had plenty of room at their halfway house for expectant mothers – it had been empty when they'd left the day before yesterday. Unless there was a pregnancy epidemic, there were enough emergency quarters for everyone.

"I have the perfect place fer all of you, and it's only an hour away," Benji announced, giving Mac a nod, making sure he knew he was part of the entourage. "We need to stop at the motel and pick up our car and our belongings, but my friends, the Melbournes, have accommodations fer up to a dozen extras if need be. They're on holiday but I'm sure they wouldn't mind. Their place can handle…"

Benji started counting heads. *My two adult daughters plus one fiancé, a grandson who I met before I even kent my wife was pregnant, and an escaped slave from one hundred and fifty years ago who I've just adopted. Explaining this explosion of the MacKay clan to the Melbournes should be interesting.*

He took a deep breath, overwhelmed with his epiphany, and said with feigned self-confidence. "I'm sure they can handle five more of my family."

"Don't forget the dog," Jane said.

"And one very large Duchess in need of a bath," Benji said. "Julianna, I take it yer familiar with driving yer fiancé's sweet ride?"

"He can sleep in the back until we get wherever we're going. I got a nap while you were out finding me another sister, so I'm good to go."

"Motel first, then directions to your place, right…Grandpa?" Mac asked, adding his now familiar pause before the designation.

Benji rolled his eyes. "Aye, but I think we need to transfer yer Aunt Daisy to the backseat of the truck. Ye see, I also remember yer grandmother's first trip in an automobile. She'd never been in anything so loud or that moved so fast."

Jane took the hint to wake up the newest member of her family. She called Daisy by name several times, finally patting her hand. "She's still out. Will one of you open the truck? I'll put her in."

"No, you won't," Mac said.

"But…but…" Jane protested.

"I'll start the truck, then you get in the backseat. I'll hand her to you. If she wakes up, she'll see you first and be less afraid," Mac said.

"Jest wonderin'," Benji said, patting the side of the huge silver crew cab truck, "Is there a reason ye rented a pickup when ye got here or did ye have a bit of warnin' and kent there was a purpose fer it?"

"I wanted something I could stretch out in," Mac said, a twinkle in his eye.

"And…" Benji prompted, knowing by the young man's sly smile that he was holding back.

"And I wanted to be prepared in case I needed a truck bed to haul something big in."

"A little heads up, eh?"

Mac shrugged. "I heard the property came with a big mangy dog. Since I knew I'd have to rent a vehicle when I got here, I figured I'd make arrangements for the mutt."

69

"Weel, after we're done here, yer more than welcome to turn in yer rental and ride with us to the Melbournes. Plenty of room fer all of us – includin' Duchess – in our van."

***

Transferring the dozing Daisy into the truck went smoothly. She stayed asleep for almost the whole trip, her head snuggled into Jane, seatbelt secured so she didn't flop forward. However, pandemonium ensued when she awoke an hour later in a strange enclosure. They had arrived at the motel parking lot and the sudden stop of movement and end of lulling road noise startled her awake.

"It's all right, it's all right," Jane said, holding Daisy close. "This is just a big carriage we're in."

Benji turned around in the front seat and told Jane, "She may not have ever seen a carriage." He turned his attention to Daisy, "We're in a big wagon with a fancy cabin built atop. See," he tapped the side window, "glass windows to let the light in and keep the bugs out. I hate bugs," he joked, shaking his head in exaggerated disgust.

Daisy's mouth twitched as she returned his smile, then she felt the restraint of the seatbelt across her chest and the fear returned.

"Unbuckle her," Mac said.

Daisy looked up at him, scared and confused at the word that sounded like a form of punishment

Jane sat forward and pressed both seatbelt buttons.

Click! Click!

The foreign sound and rapid movement of nylon across her body sent Daisy scrambling into Jane's lap, her weight not much more than a child's.

"It's all right. We won't let anything hurt you," Jane comforted. "Any of us. Just remember, this is tomorrow. Nobody owns anyone else here. You're safe."

"No masters or boss men?" Daisy asked.

"Weel," Benji said, "not like when yer from. We still have people we call bosses, but we can walk away anytime we want. No one has the right to be my master or yours or his or hers, though," he added, pointing to each in turn.

Jane felt Daisy relax at Benji's assurance. "We'll take care of you," Jane said, giving her a quick hug.

"Aye, yer family now – our family," Benji said. "I'll go in and grab a few of our goods. This is an inn. We'll get ye somethin' to eat and then take ye home. At least, our home until a new one is built."

Jane felt Daisy's body tense in confusion. "I think we'll wait out here. I'd like to take her inside and give her a shower to clean up her wounds, but I think treating an infection would be easier than explaining all the newness. Would one of you run across the street and get a to-go order of rice? Maybe with a full belly, she'll fall back asleep."

They heard a whistle – two shorts and a long, just like Benji used – and looked out the window. Julianna stood outside, a white paper bag in her hand and a huge smile on her face. "I got her lunch," she said. When Benji leaned forward, ready to roll down the window, she said, "Don't!"

He opened the door instead. "Why not? And how'd ye get food so fast?"

"First, the window rolling down – growling and disappearing into the door – would have scared her, I'm sure. Second, I ordered ahead. I knew where we were coming, so got on my phone and found the nearest Chinese food restaurant. I paid with a debit card, drove through, and *Voila!* Dinner for my new sister."

"That was mighty considerate of ye," Benji said, taking the food from her. He opened the bag and held up the spork that was inside. "I guess she can start adapting to the twenty-first century right away."

"Hmph!"

Julianna stepped aside at the familiar grunt of derision coming from behind her. "What's the matter with you?" she asked Mali.

"This isn't over yet," Mali said, searching the streets. "If she had one coin, there were more."

"So?" Benji asked. "What is it yer not tellin' us?"

"He's trying to get all of them. He wants to corner the market on those coins. There's new technology available for time travel, but it's buggy. Silver drachmas are still the only safe way."

"Buggy?" Jane asked. "I know what bugs are, but what does buggy mean?"

"It means there are problems with it," Mac said, then turned back to Mali. "Mom, we're all family, so tell us. Are you behind the missing coins?"

"Yeah, well, sort of," she said, looking down at her hands.

"By the way yer not making eye contact with anyone," Benji said, "I'd say yer the one who started this whole mess."

Mali's head popped up; her confidence returned. "I had to. Or at least, someone had to take the coins from him. He was – is – chaos personified."

"According to Greek mythology, Chaos wasna a person but the void that was the beginning of time," Benji said. "Are ye sure ye don't mean Loki, the Norse god of mischief?"

"Yeah, that's closer. He called himself the son of Loki. I didn't believe him, though. He's more than mischief. He really is chaos…and greedy, evil, deceiving…"

"And my father," Mac said. "Thanks."

"Hey, it's not your fault! I mean," Mali said, and then her stalwart demeanor began to crumble. "I couldn't abort you. You were my child. I didn't know about *it* until later."

"What? The legend that the child of Red Storm would be his demise?" Mac asked.

She nodded.

"Would it have made a difference?"

"No," she said. "I had the choice – you or him – and I chose you. I thought I loved him, but that went away when I saw he wanted to create havoc, not just watch it. I decided to leave after he wouldn't let me stop the big oil spill in Alaska. I stole one of his coins, hid the rest, then slipped to 2032.

"I couldn't come back to Mom and Da, a pregnant runaway. I moved every month until you were born. January 31, 2033. A New Year's baby."

"I know. Chinese New Year. The Year of the Ox. You tell me that every birthday. At least, all that you were around for," Mac growled, suddenly angry all over again at being abandoned.

Mali pointed her index finger at him. "Not now, son. I've told you, I did it to save you. But I was there for the first ten, almost eleven birthdays. When I saw that sweet face of yours for the first time, I knew I'd do whatever it took – even giving you up – if it would keep you safe and away from him. All the running around we did, moving every six months, was hard, but I couldn't watch you die or know that I'd been careless and the reason he'd found you."

"I don't think you have to worry about that anymore. He doesn't know I'm here, in this time. Besides, we're moving – again. Speaking of which, I'm turning in my keys to the rental truck, then riding with my grandparents. I'll see you at their place. If you decide to show up."

Benji watched the young man give his mother her comeuppance, surprised that he had so much restraint, then chuckled to himself. Yes, whether he was furious at her or not, he wouldn't make a scene in front of the woman he was trying to impress. He leaned into the truck and saw Daisy had given up on the spork and was eating the last few grains of rice out of the paper container with her deft, slender fingers, her eyes flitting to the side under her long eyelashes, watching Mac without being obvious. Smitten.

"Grandpa," Mac called out, getting his attention. "Let's clean out our rooms then swap the females over to your van."

"Nah," Benji said. "I think we should do it the other way around. I'm parked over there. See if Duchess will come with ye, and I'll get yer grandma and new aunt transferred."

"Ergh," Mac grumbled softly, then whispered, "If you don't mind, Grandpa, don't call her my aunt. At least, around me. It feels…"

"Uncomfortable? Unnatural? Unsettling?" Benji asked, grinning.

"All of the above."

"Aye, I'll see if I can get Janie and Daisy settled into the van while ye transfer all yer personal goods and the dog."

"Thanks," Mac said, then put his hand on Benji's shoulder. "I mean it. Grandpa."

"Yer welcome. Grandson."

Chapter 13

Jane offered her hand to Daisy, helping her out of the truck. For the first time, the young woman brought up her chin and looked at the world around her. Her knees started to buckle, but Jane had anticipated it. Or rather, suspected Daisy would either falter or run. Gratefully, it was the former. She didn't know if she could catch up to her if she did bolt. Probably, since her legs were so much longer than Daisy's – but she didn't want to call attention to either one of them. The last thing they needed was to have the police involved. Daisy was scared, minimally dressed, and had no identification. There was one other thing she didn't have: a last name. In less than two hours, life got very complicated.

"Daisy, look at me." When she remained frozen in terror, Jane tried again, this time, her arm around the woman's shoulder – holding her close despite the heat – walking with her. "If you look at me, you won't see anything else. Remember, I promised we wouldn't let anyone or anything hurt you."

Jane could feel a slight lessening of tension in Daisy's shoulder, but her head was still down and her reluctance to proceed showed in her slowing pace.

"Daisy, would you rather go back to Master Joe and Boss Man?"

She straightened up and faced Jane at the words, wide-eyed and obedient. "I'll look at you. No go back. Please."

"Then trust me," Jane said. "Yes, it's going to be scary, at least for a few days." She pushed the remote and opened up the van from fifteen feet away so fresh air would blow through, replacing the trapped heat of the day.

"This is a car," she said when they got to it. "A van. This is how people travel long distances without horses or mules. These go fast but are safe. Like a wagon, you'll feel the bumps in the road sometimes, but I'll be here with you."

Jane watched Daisy's eyebrows rise as her focus shifted, looking for something. No, not something – someone.

Mac.

"Mac will be with us, too. And my husband, and the dog, and maybe Mali. The other man, Silas, and his woman will be in the other car. The one you were sitting in at the house."

"The custard-colored porch with windows?" Daisy asked.

"Porch?" Jane thought for a moment. "Yes, it's like a porch with seats and doors and a roof, but it moves like the truck."

"Truck?"

"Truck, car, van: they're all vehicles…" Jane explained and saw she was losing her.

Benji came up and stood by the open door. "Not as easy as it seems, is it, dear?" he said with a chuckle.

"How soon we adapt and forget," Jane said. "The worst is yet to come, though: starting the motor."

Benji shook his head and grinned. "Nae. If I recall, ye were scared most of the fast vehicles zoomin' past us."

Jane rolled her eyes. "Do you happen to have an extra bandana? I used both of mine to make a blouse for her."

Benji reached into his back pocket, confused but obeying and not asking why. "Oh," he said, "like a blindfold fer a mule. Jest be sure she kens yer doing it out of concern fer her."

Daisy eyed the dark blue cloth Benji offered her. "You understand what we're talking about, don't you?"

Daisy nodded.

"Then here." Jane put it in her hand. "Put it on whenever you'd like."

Daisy shook the handkerchief out and folded it into a triangle, quickly and efficiently reconfiguring it into a blindfold, and put it on immediately.

"Ready?" Jane asked.

Daisy nodded, her hands now folded in her lap.

"I don't think I want to ken how she learned to do that so well," Benji said.

"A slave's secrets aren't readily – or willingly – shared," Jane said. "Sometimes, they're all they have."

***

"Mali decided to ride with Silas and Julianna," Mac said, leading Duchess into the van with the collar-leash combination he had made out of his belt. He stepped in behind the dog and settled onto the center bench seat, then turned sideways so he could see Daisy. He looked up at the rearview mirror and made eye contact with Benji in the driver's seat. "In other words, we're ready to rock this world."

"Rock this world?" Benji asked. "Do you mean rock and roll?"

"If that's how you say 'let's jet,' then yes, let's go. You all may be used to this heat, but a little artificially created environment would be appreciated."

"Ye'll have to live with the windows rolled down. Daisy will freeze with the a/c on."

"Yes, and she'll piss herself if she feels the wind rushing past her," Mac countered.

"Point taken," Benji said. "Windows shut, air conditioning set to a balmy eighty-five degrees."

Mac leaned sideways and wiped his sweaty brow on his shoulder. "I'll accept that compromise."

Benji turned the ignition and not only the engine roared to life, but the stereo did, too. "…I believe in yesterday…"

Click.

"Sorry about that," Benji said. "I forgot it was on."

"An appropriate song," Mac said, then turned around. "How's she doing, Granny?"

"Better than I expected. I guess the blindfold was a good idea." Jane turned her attention to Daisy. "Are you all right, sweetie?"

Daisy nodded, then held her hand to her mouth.

"Or not," Jane said.

Mac saw the impending loss of lunch and quickly dumped the contents of his shopping bag onto the seat beside him, snack wrappers, and granola bars scattering. "Just in case."

"I'll take the highway," Benji said. "It's not only faster, but the roads are straighter. Janie, I ken she's afraid, but watching the horizon works to get rid of motion sickness both on land and sea."

"Give us a minute," Jane said, then started humming the song her mother used to sing to her when she was frightened. "You'll be fine. I've got you," she cooed to Daisy.

"Bonding," Mac said softly.

"Ahem."

Mac looked up at the rearview mirror and saw Benji trying to get his attention. "Yes?" he asked.

"She needs a mother, not a *special* friend," Benji said.

Mac grinned at him. "I'm not going anywhere."

Benji raised one eyebrow in answer, then looked back at the road.

76

"At least for a while," Mac said, then added, "if ever."

Benji caught his eye in the mirror again. "Kind of fond of the early twenty-first century, are ye?"

Mac chuckled. "You don't know how great you have it," he said. "No idea at all. And that's a good thing."

***

Two minutes into the drive, Daisy had fallen asleep again, the top half of her slumped over, cradled in Jane's arms. Benji looked up and saw the cuddled-up duo. "Ye look so natural holdin' a babe, even if she is nearly yer age."

Jane chuckled and nodded to Mac. "Something as simple as knowing our birthdays would be a treasure to either one of us," she said, looking down at Daisy. "She may not even know how old she is. If she's been traded or sold several times, the age given was to increase her value. Mac, you lost your mother when you were almost eleven, but she's here now. I didn't get that second chance, and I doubt Daisy did, either. Please, let your mother back into your life."

Mac remained mute, jaws clenched. Benji glanced at him in the mirror. "She did say it was to keep ye safe, aye?"

"Yeah, she did. I guess it worked, too. I mean, I'm here. I hated being at that boarding school. When she didn't return my calls or emails after I'd been there for two weeks, I realized what she'd done. I ran away once but came back before they even know I'd split. One look at the kids downtown eating out of dumpsters was enough to change my mind."

"Dumpsters?" Jane asked.

"Trash bins," Benji clarified, then added, "I've done that more than once in my youth." He paused. "And quite a few times after I grew up. When yer hungry, the serving platter doesna make much difference."

Thump!

The van lurched forward. Jane clutched Daisy closer, whispering, "I got you," to the startled woman, trying to calm herself at the same time.

Thump!

The van careened with the impact, the right side slipping off the pavement onto the soft shoulder of crushed rock.

Benji gripped the steering wheel and held on, his knuckles white and biceps bulging as he steadied the van, bringing all four wheels back onto the roadway from its brief lopsided sprint down the mismatched surfaces. He looked in the rearview mirror but couldn't see anyone. The culprit had either left the highway or was below his line of sight, invisible to him with tailing so close.

Thump!

He was back. The fiend was more than tailgating – he was practically up-his-exhaust pipe-ing!

Benji floored the accelerator to put distance between him and the idiot behind him, checking the road ahead for a safety turnout or oncoming traffic that might be in the way. "Can ye see who or what it is, Mac?"

Mac turned sideways in the seat. "He's too close. Can you change lanes or speed up?"

Benji quickly turned the wheel, driving into the oncoming lane, then came back just as fast. It worked. The yellow Camaro behind him hadn't anticipated the maneuver. "It's the same car, all right," Mac said. "The one we played chicken with."

"Here's hopin' he doesna ken these roads as well as I do. Now he's in my backyard."

"Don't play with him," Mac said. "I never met the man, but he's trying to get you to go faster or drive recklessly. That's *not* what you want to do." He turned around and saw Jane and Daisy were wide-eyed and nauseous. "Slow down and see if he'll pass."

Benji let off the accelerator and received an immediate *thump*.

"Keep slowing down…" Mac said.

"If ye say so, but first…" Benji sped up just a bit then pulled to the right, anticipating the emergency lane he knew was just ahead. He took his foot off the accelerator and watched the side mirror.

The Camaro was letting off!

"Looks like ye were right," Benji said, then looked again.

The Camaro had sped up and was now beside him. The red-haired driver in mirrored sunglasses grinned broadly at him, his perfect white teeth shining like an ad for toothpaste. His lips suddenly puckered into a tight-jawed scowl of malintent and he leaned forward.

"Watch out!" Mac hollered, recognizing his own expression of impending wrath.

Benji had also seen the emotional shift and was ready. He steered into the passing lane and stomped on the brake, decelerating sharply but not stopping. The Camaro with the mangled front end almost sped past him.

Almost.

Storm was pacing them now. Everyone in the van got a good look at him, but it was Jane who brought up her smartphone and began shooting a video, getting documentation on the man who had no written history, no known photo. The man who had stolen her daughter from her.

The posturing was violent now. No longer bumper thumps, Storm was cutting the wheel, ramming the right front of his car into Benji, glaring at him, trying to get him to lose emotional control.

"Mom said Storm feeds on other people's fear and rage," Mac said. "She said it wasn't a challenge for him unless he got a strong emotional reaction from his victims."

At the last *thunk,* Benji turned and looked at Storm.

Storm threw off his glasses and stared. *It's Mali's father, not her son!* He looked toward the back of the van and saw another redhead, looking back at him with anger. *But there's her son. No, not just her son, my son. He looks so much like I did at that age...*

The dust mote of compassion disappeared. Whether they looked alike or not, he would get rid of him. Take out the son who was prophesized to be his own demise.

Wrath reinvigorated, Storm cut the wheel again, accelerating into the side of the van, pushing with a steady force to deliver a death ride off the side of the mountain. No more lambasts of intimidation. It was time for the finale.

Evasive maneuvers he'd used when racing sprint cars flashed through Benji's mind. He shuffled through the possibilities, but all were reckless. He couldn't use any of them, not with his wife and family in the car. He let off the accelerator and felt the force of the powerful Chevy move him to the right, closer to the shoulder. Using all his might, he steered into his assailant, strong-arming the wheel to keep the van from being pushed into the gorge below. It wasn't working, though. He was barely able to keep the wheels turned the right direction. He sped up and turned left, hoping for a gap between the vehicles so *he* could be the battering ram and give Storm a taste of his own unwanted attention – so *he* could be the assailant, not the victim.

And there it was. The break he'd been waiting for – the loss of metal to metal contact between the two cars. "Hold on!" Benji shouted and stomped on the brakes. Tires smoked and squealed as the antilock brakes held true. The van skidded in a straight path – no fishtailing or Ferris-wheel-spinning out of control.

They all watched open-mouthed as the canary yellow Camaro sped past them, a huge, vintage Cadillac pushing it down the road, a familiar-looking dark-skinned woman waving and smiling out the back window at them.

Benji pulled off the road into a cleared area, an entrance to a logging road. "Was that…?" he asked.

"Yeah, I think that was my mother," Mac said. "Looks like Silas skipped the nap. Apparently, he has a few driving skills, too."

"Plus, just as much – if not more – horsepower as the Camaro and a lot more mass," Benji said, backing up to get in position to hit the road again.

"And a set this big," Mac added, holding up both hands as if holding cantaloupes. "*Huevos grandes.*"

"Is it over?" Jane asked, ignoring the crude comment. She didn't speak whatever language Mac was babbling in, but the gesture of 'big balls' was clear enough.

Benji began to say, "Yes," but was cut off by Mac.

"I doubt it."

Benji scowled at Mac, silently reproving him for frightening the women.

"I'm not going to lie to anyone," Mac said. "He's either going to hang back and get a new plan, or Silas is falling into a trap. Either way, the one thing he doesn't expect is for us to follow him – to be a back up for our back up."

"Are ye sayin' we should go lookin' fer trouble?" Benji asked.

"No, I'm saying Silas just saved us. We should return the favor. You don't want to lose both of your daughters before they're even born, do you?"

Jane and Benji gasped and Daisy sat up straight, her mouth slack in confusion.

"Don't worry about it," Jane soothed, then kissed the top of her head. "It's a tomorrow and today thing. You don't need to understand." She thought a moment and added, "And we definitely don't talk to anyone outside of the family about any of this. Not everyone can go from today to yesterday or tomorrow. As a matter of fact, most folks don't believe it's even possible."

"And if you *did* say anything, they'd probably put you in a rubber room," Mac added.

Daisy reached up and gently put her index finger over her lips, showing she understood the need to stay silent, then sank back into her protector, Jane. She didn't say a word, but her face showed it: she didn't know what a rubber room was, but I didn't want to find out, either.

***

Two miles ahead, the crew spotted Silas standing in front of his Cadillac, Julianna and Mali stepping out of the vehicle to join him.

Benji pulled up behind them, and he and Mac got out. "What's going on?" Mac asked before Benji had the chance. He looked over at his grandfather and shrugged a shoulder. *Sorry. Bossiness and taking charge is part of my nature, too.*

Silas looked at Benji first, grinned at the irony, and then back at Mac. "Looks like your father is going to find out if he's part duck."

"Sire," Benji and Mac chorused, both correcting Silas at the same time.

Mac glanced at Benji, his eyes bright with gratitude at the dismissal of the familial title, then back to the water. The bright yellow Camaro was swiftly sinking, disappearing into the lake that stretched for acres alongside the road. Sopping wet with red hair covering half his face, Storm was struggling to climb out through the window. His sunglasses slipped down his face and he quickly pushed them back up only to find that one arm was broken and they wouldn't stay put. Ignoring his audience, he grasped them and flung them away.

Mac watched where they landed and quickly snapped a picture of the area. He knew those weren't ordinary sunglasses. Hopefully, Storm wasn't thinking clearly and wouldn't be back to retrieve them. They were synced to Storm's server – not his – but he could make a few modifications and access the information on both the sunglasses and in Storm's cloud account. No telling what secrets were kept there.

Silas put his foot on the twisted strip of aluminum in front of him that had failed to stop Storm's speeding car. On impact, it had ripped away from the post. The stump of rotted wood was now broken off at ground level. "They should have replaced these guardrails years ago," he said. "These aren't even treated lumber. Oh, and sorry about the misnomer. I knew he was never around to be a father."

81

"Well," Mac said, inhaling to push down his conflicted emotions, "it looks like he's not in any danger. He can hitch a ride to wherever he's going. If he had wanted to talk to us, he would have approached us in a different way. Grandpa?" He paused and looked at Benji, waiting for eye contact before he proceeded.

"Yes…Grandson," he replied.

"If you'd do the honors of leading the way to your place, we'd appreciate it. I think we've all had enough excitement for today."

Benji glanced at Silas, then answered Mac, "The day's still young, but I agree; it's time to hit the road."

"Come on, ladies," Silas called, his arms wide to gather his fiancée and soon-to-be sister-in-law. "Let's leave this soggy Swede to make his own way back to land and transportation."

"Nutso Norse Viking," Mali corrected, then added, "but I agree. He's never asked for nor wanted anyone's help. I doubt he's changed."

***

Twenty minutes later, Benji pushed the button in the ceiling console on the van, opening the garage door. The roar and clank-clank of the motor and chain mechanism startled Daisy, and a small, "Eek!" slipped out before she squeezed her mouth shut and eyes tight, pulling the bandana back.

Waiting to drive in, Benji paused, signaling for Silas to take the open parking spot next to him.

When the men were out and the women had disentangled themselves from seatbelts and backseats, Benji explained, "The lady of the house is gone for a week or so. Even if she were here, Bibb would be open to havin' more guests. She runs a home for ladies in waiting."

He glanced over at Mali. "Now, if I didn't explain it to ye before – when ye were in need – I'm tellin' ye now. Babies happen. They don't always wait on the plannin' part of bein' a family. Just over a year ago, I helped bring Bibb's vision of a home for unwed mothers to wall and window form. This is a safe spot fer women of any age who finds herself in a family way. Whether she doesna have a home, or her home isna safe, or she jest wants to be discreet, she can stay here. The young ladies can also get schoolin' or learn a trade here while they're waitin' fer the bairn to be born if they desire. They all help around the house. Or rather, home. It's their temporary family manse."

Mali snorted at the lecture that was over twenty years late. Or too early. *If he ever told me about this before, I ignored it. Just like the majority of advice he gave me.*

"I'm sorry, Da," she said. She stepped over and gave him a big – and sincere – hug. "I don't know why I was so resistant to everything you said. I think I wanted to do everything my way."

Benji rolled his eyes at her remark, remembering how he had faked his own death to 'spare' his parents paying a ransom to the men who had kidnapped him. How would life have turned out if he had let them take charge of the situation? There was no telling, but he probably wouldn't have wound up with Janie as his wife if he had.

"Ye never ken why ye make a rash decision. Or decisions. I'm sure it seemed the right thing to do at the time though, aye?"

Mali paused and thought about that day. *Yes, it had seemed like the right choice. The only one possible if I was to be with Storm. There was no way Da would let me leave home as a minor with a professional time traveler!*

"Yes, it felt right at the time," she admitted sheepishly.

"As a parent, would ye let yer daughter – or son – leave like ye did?" Benji cocked his head in the direction they had just come from. "With someone like him?"

"No!" she said, then realized what he was doing. "And stop using your damned logic to trap me into feeling guilty about making a rotten choice. *That's* why I left!"

Chapter 14

"If you don't mind," Jane said, addressing the two older women she was beginning to accept as her daughters, "I'd like to show Daisy around here by myself and in my own way."

"Sounds reasonable," Mali said.

"Especially since you're the only one with that kind of experience," Julianna answered.

"Coming forward in time a hundred and fifty years," Mali said, picking up and verbalizing the rest of the thread.

"Except it was over two hundred years for Mama," Julianna corrected. She felt rather than saw the glare of reproach from her older sister and softened her unintentional rebuke. "Anything over a hundred years is going to be looney, no matter how you do the math."

"Looney?" Jane asked.

"Awkward and confusing," Julianna said. "Sorry. We'll just leave you two alone."

Mali bumped elbows with her sister. "Come on. We'll let Da give us the grand tour."

The two left the room, leaving Jane with Daisy, still blindfolded.

Jane reached up and touched the knot, ready to untie it and begin her education about twenty-first-century life.

Daisy cringed and asked, "Do you have to?"

"Well, I'm glad you're speaking up for yourself now," she said, moving her hand away. "That's a very big step, but I think you can handle seeing what's around here. Your first experience with riding in a car was scary. Normally, it isn't dangerous. Cars rarely bump into each other like that. At least, on purpose."

"All right then," Daisy said and took off the bandana. She blinked her eyes rapidly at the brightness, then sighed. Everything looked shiny and colorful, but the table and chairs weren't so different from what she was used to. She saw the array of cast iron pots hanging from hooks and felt more comfortable. The cotton print curtains on the windows looked familiar. She glanced down and saw the silvery metal device above the large washbasin and gasped how elaborate the hand pump was.

Jane picked up Daisy's hand and patted it. "Let's do this a little bit at a time. I don't know if you realize it, but I came from more yesterdays than you did. I grew up when your great-great-grandmother was a child. Or maybe it was just one great."

"Was that before the time of telegraphs?" Daisy asked.

"I'm sorry," Jane said. "I know what a telephone is, but not a telegraph."

"It's a way to talk to someone without speaking. But it isn't slow like sending a letter. The words are sent and received real fast. Master Joe had one so he could talk to folks far away about the war," Daisy said.

"Oh, we have something like that now. It's called email. But no, we didn't have telephones or anything else like that when I came from." Jane picked up the remote for the ceiling fan, then decided that would be too much too soon. "Let's start with indoor plumbing. We have a privy and bath in one room here. Oh, and we don't have to heat the water over a fire. It comes out of the wall that way."

"Water out of a wall?"

Jane led Daisy into the bathroom and opened the cabinet under the sink. She pointed to the pipes and explained, "Water comes into the house through these. Most of them are behind the wall. They have a way to heat it before it comes out." She saw how shocked Daisy was. "Now I know what Benji went through. There's nothing like the first time, right?" she said, not expecting an answer.

"Excuse me," Daisy asked reluctantly. "If there's no privy, where do you…um…do your business?"

"Oh! Yes, that was confusing to me, too. See this here," Jane said, lifting up the toilet seat. "You sit down, do your business, use this to wipe yourself…but not too much." She pulled off a length of toilet paper. "Then throw it into the toilet bowl when you're done and flush."

Jane pushed the handle down, startling Daisy with the sudden rush of water. "The flow of water takes the waste away from the house somewhere. We never have to worry about that part. So, since it's been a hot and sticky day, I'll draw you a bath, then get some clothes picked out for you." She looked up at Daisy's short-cropped hair. "At least that part will be easy to take care of."

Daisy noticed her staring at her hair. "Bossman wanted to count me as one of his men, trying to fool Master Joe. You see, one of the slaves runned away. But Master Joe is smart man. He remembered me by my face, not my hair or the man's clothes Bossman told me to wear." Daisy brought her hands up to her mouth and giggled. "I think Master Joe broke his crop on Bossman, switching him for lying to him."

"Well, no one here is going to make you look like a man. Women can wear trousers if they'd like. You already saw clothes are different. Just remember..." Jane said and waited for Daisy to speak.

Daisy looked side to side, her dumbfounded look turning into a grin. "I'm safe and everyone here will take care of me."

"And no whips, either."

"And no whips," she repeated, genuinely happy for the first time in forever.

***

Daisy flinched and swallowed a yelp but didn't cower from the noise of the tub faucet turning on.

Jane put her hand in the flow of water, checking the temperature. "Put your hand here," she said.

Seeing that it looked harmless and certain that Jane wouldn't hurt or trick her, Daisy checked the flow of the endless bucket loads of water spurting from the wall through what looked like a metal gate handle.

"And when you're done," Jane explained, "you call me. This plug is a little tricky. You'll get the hang of it soon. After all, you do plan on staying here for a while, right?"

"A while?" Daisy asked, untying a side knot in her bandana shirt.

"Sure. We'll get you caught up with what's new in this time, teach you to read and do your numbers, and get used to your new life. Maybe you want to get a job..." Jane stopped when Daisy tensed.

"What's wrong? You can wait until I'm gone to get in," Jane said. "I really didn't think you'd be bashful."

"Bashful? No, not bashful. I don't want to get a job if I have to go to a different house."

"No, no, that's not what I mean." Jane pointed to the tub. "Get in and we'll talk."

Daisy pulled at the half-hitch knot in her rope belt and her flour-sack skirt dropped to the floor, her blue handkerchief blouse right on top of it. She stepped into the tub. "So much water! It feels so good." She scooted forward and lay back, submerging her head in the rapidly filling tub, then shot back up, terrified.

"Oh, that's just the noise of the water pouring into the tub," Jane explained. "It's sort of like hearing nuts falling down on the buckets you wear on your head during harvest. Nothing is going to hurt you. Now, let me lather up this cloth and wash your back. Then I'll explain going to work at an office or store and coming home later in the day. That's how most people do it now. They don't work from home."

Daisy reached up and placed her hand on Jane's arm. "I never want to leave you. You're my home."

"Daisy, yes, this is your home for now. But later, you might find a place that's nicer for you. Better for what you want to do with your life. You can do anything in this time, especially once you've learned reading, writing, and numbers. You get money from working. And you can own land, property, and even a house. And a car."

"No, no – I don't want a car. I'll walk."

"I don't think that's going to work out too well, but we don't have to worry about that for now." Jane paused at the voices. Mac, Benji, and Silas were laughing loudly, joking about something, only bits of their conversation coming through the bathroom window. "Besides, you might meet the right man and want to get married. That's why I'm here. I met the right man in my yesterday. He wanted to marry me right away but couldn't because of the color of my skin. Rather than stay there and live with me as his slave, he brought me here, to my tomorrow."

Jane winced as she gently scrubbed at the superficial wounds on Daisy's back, sympathizing at the pain but glad they weren't deep or infected. When she was done, she dipped a cup in the tub and rinsed her. "It was scary – very scary – at first. Here," she said, handing her the soap and washcloth, "you can reach everything else. I guess the scariness is about the same for both of us. The difference is that you have me to explain this tomorrow world instead of a man who wants to marry you."

Daisy bowed her head at the words, bringing the cloth to her face to hide her grin of excitement. *Maybe Mac wants to marry me. Maybe that's why he smiles at me.* She inhaled the scent of the washcloth. *And I'll be clean and smell pretty for him, too.*

Chapter 15

Jane dressed Daisy in one of her own simple but colorful cotton shifts – bright yellow with orange butterflies. What went to her knees was an ankle-length gown on the much shorter woman. She didn't bother offering any undergarments, knowing the contemporary small clothes would confuse the slave who had probably never worn any.

"Now how do you feel?" Jane asked, although by the radiant smile on the rescued woman's face, she could tell Daisy had benefitted greatly from the bath.

Once shut in fear, her eyes were now wide with wonder as she took in the tidy room Jane had told her would be her apartment. Inhaling deeply, she took in all aspects of the clean white walls, the framed painting of her namesake flower over the large mattress covered with clean bedding. The fineness of the sheer curtains that covered real glass windows, solid and polished tile floors instead of packed earth or twice-used straw fascinated her. She'd probably never seen a room so elegant. And it was hers to use. "I'm sorry," Daisy said. "Did you say something?"

"No, not really," Jane replied. "I was just commenting about how quickly you're adjusting. Let's go check on the others, shall we?"

Jane stuck her head in the kitchen, Daisy close behind, holding her hand. "Something smells good," Jane said, sniffing the air, trying to identify the aroma.

Benji chuckled. "I'm a fair cook, but Silas asked if he could be in charge of our meal."

"And of course, being the great host, you agreed," Jane replied. She changed her focus to the silver-haired savior of the day and her forty-something-year-old daughters, skittering around with plates and silverware as Benji rearranged chairs at the table. "And it looks like he has a few volunteers."

"It's not as if they have anythin' else to do," Benji said, then winked at them. They returned his sassiness with identical frowns. "Ye do look alike. And quite a bit like yer mother. I suppose no blood test is necessary. I believe revealing birthdates may be a bit complicated, so I think we may have to do a little creative writing." He looked back at Jane and tipped his head. "Again."

Mali glanced at Julianna and winked with the same bright glint her father had given her. Julianna noticed her father's scowl of confusion and explained. "We both have multiple IDs. One of the first things we do when we get to a new time is go to the DMV and give them 'the look.'" Both girls looked at him with identical pouts, bottom lips pouched out in feigned sorrow.

Mali continued. "Yeah, we didn't know we both had the same routine. That's one of the things we were talking about when we were up in the trees this morning."

"About that..." Benji asked, his eyebrows crowded. "Why were ye there?"

"To see you and Mom," they said at the same time. They looked at each other and laughed at their reply. Their identical giggles caused heartier snorts which resulted in more boisterous noises, their sequence of laughs echoing one another, all the same tone, duration, and at the same time.

"Are ye sure ye aren't twins?" he asked.

"Only if there was an eighteen-month delay in delivery," Julianna said.

"Probably," Mali added, giving her sister a playful punch to the shoulder. "You're late for everything."

"We both knew the date you bought the manse and the story about the explosion, so were sure you'd be safe. But if we popped in, we'd be changing things and someone could have been hurt."

"Because we weren't in that original timeline, we figured we'd wait until the poof!" Mali said, moving her hands in and out to illustrate the big bang that had blown outward and then turned in on itself. "After the implosion was finished, we'd come over and say hi."

"Or something like that," Julianna added, unsure of herself. "We hadn't worked out the details. I mean, it's not as if we had a plan."

"Or even knew the other would show up..."

"It just seems to happen that way. Or at least it used to when we were in the same time."

"Looks like we still have it though, right, Sis?" Mali asked, forgoing a wink, and instead smiled broadly.

Benji, Jane and Daisy, Silas and Mac had been following their rapid conversation like a championship tennis match, heads tracking from one to the other as they finished each other's thoughts and sentences.

"And why did ye finally decide to come back?" Benji asked. "Not that I dinna mind meetin' ye both, but I thought yer mother and I would do it the traditional way, feelin' ye grow in her womb, watchin' ye day by day after ye popped out…"

The two women looked at each other, blinking. "Um, I don't know, do you?" Mali asked Julianna.

"Well, yeah. I finally had someone who believed me about time travel. I kinda, sorta wanted him to meet my parents. This is the only stable time I knew to bring him. Well, that and it was close by. You know, slipping from 2010 forward to 2015? That wasn't too much of a hop. Besides, he found a couple of coins." She sidled up to Silas and put her arm around his waist, his arm automatically opening up to hold her. "This guy can track anything!"

"You wanted me to meet your parents?" Silas asked, grinning. "Was there a special reason why?"

"Well, first off, I wanted to make sure you weren't just humoring me. I didn't think so. I mean, some of this open-mindedness stuff is genetic. Your granddaughter – at least the one triplet, Tori – believed me. I didn't talk to the others about it. Everyone thinks she's a little looney, but she's just extra sharp. Like you." Julianna leaned over and kissed him on the cheek, making him blush.

"And you figured if there was something evil about me, your father – whose judgment you trusted – would see it?" Silas asked, for the first time in his life enjoying the sudden warmth of his rosy cheeks.

"Not right or wrong…" she said. She swished her pursed lips back and forth, trying to find the words. "Make no mistake about it; I love you just like you are. You're perfect as far as I'm concerned. If you were here, I was sure Da would see if you were deceiving me. However, one look at your face when you found out we really were five years ahead of where we started told me what I needed to know. But, you *knew* we'd get here, right?"

"No doubt in my mind," he said. "Still, I'm glad you cared enough about me to introduce me to your parents. Even if a tad bit early in the relationship," he added with a chuckle.

Benji rolled his eyes and Jane shook her head with a smile, then looked his way. She could tell her husband agreed with her. Silas was a good man. "So, what smells so good?" she asked.

Daisy dipped her head and brought her hand to her face, sniffing the lingering floral scent. Rich people soap, not the harsh mushy lye that was allotted the slaves. If they ever got any at all. She stood up tall, remembering she was free now.

Jane saw Daisy's gesture and amended her question. "What's for lunch? It smells great."

Benji returned to watching Mac again. His grandson's gaze had left Daisy only briefly while his mother and her sister had been jabbering. A big grin rose on the young redhead's face. Benji looked at Daisy to see why. She had pulled her shoulders back. She was standing tall and proud, an underfed young woman of indeterminate age but definitely a full-grown woman. She was also watching Mac out of the corner of her eye like Jane used to watch him – and still did at times. Apparently, Mac now had a reason *not* to go back to the future. Maybe he'd have help building his new home. The girls – mature women, he reminded himself – had referred to it as the MacKay Manse. He'd have to start with a lot more than two bedrooms if that was the case.

"Coq au vin," Silas said. "Everything needed was here and Benji assured me it was all right to use the wine."

"I'm more of a beer or cider man myself," Benji said. "The wine was a gift. I'm glad you could make use of it."

"While this good man is preparing the meal, I have a quick errand to run," Mac said, his gaze cutting to the door, then pausing on Daisy. "I'll be back in a flash."

"But…but…" Mali stammered. "You just got here."

"And so did you. I won't be more than a nano."

"Huh?" Benji sputtered.

"Nanosecond," Mac explained. "Well, more than that, but I wouldn't leave if it wasn't time-sensitive. Just trust me."

"Do ye need a hand?"

"Maybe. Yeah, come along. Grandpa."

Benji gave Jane a quick hug and kiss. "We'll be right back. You got this, right?"

Jane looked at Daisy and her two daughters, now standing together. "Like jumping in a lake to learn how to swim, aye? Yes, I think I can handle diving into motherhood."

"Plus, she has me here to help," Silas said, coming to stand next to her with ladle in hand. "Right, Mother Jane?" he added with a friendly wink.

She frowned in confusion, then brightened up as she realized the man who was at least twice, maybe three times her age, was going to be her son-in-law. "Right, son."

Chapter 16

"I'll drive, if you don't mind," Mac said, heading to the driver's side.

"As long as ye ken where yer goin' and how to drive this beast," Benji replied. "Although with the size of the rig ye were drivin' earlier, I'd say this bitty pony willna be much of a challenge."

Mac caught the keys tossed to him and stuck them in his pocket. He hated to leave the party but didn't want to lose the daylight. Or chance Storm being there. Hopefully, that vain sire of a bastard son or two wanted to get cleaned up and acquire a new spiffy ride before being seen in public. For some people, image was everything. And from what his mother had told him, Storm was the poster child for Primo Dons. If there was such a group.

"Let me check something first." Mac slid into the driver's seat and sighed in comfort. For once, he didn't have to adjust for his long legs. He picked up his phone, selected the image he had taken of where Storm had tossed his sunglasses in a hissy fit, zoomed in with the finder icon, and selected the 'take me there' option. He set the device in the cupholder and said, "Alexis, use voice directions." He didn't think he'd meet anyone else on the road, but he certainly didn't want to take the chance that someone would see the holographic image floating in front of the windshield as he drove down the road. He couldn't remember when that option was released but was certain it wasn't available in 2015. He got by with it earlier but didn't want to push his luck.

"Start," he said, then waited and said, "Ignition." When the car didn't turn on, he huffed. "Damn. I must be more tired than I thought." He took the small keyfob out of his pocket, stuck the key into the slot in the dash, and turned it. "How quaint."

Benji remained mute for the ride, not wanting to disturb Mac's concentration as he followed the audible prompts from his fancy phone. Before too long, they were at the site of the earlier fracas. "Do ye need a hand?" he asked.

"No," Mac said, then made a slight grunting noise as he changed his mind. "Yes. Keep an eye out and make sure someone doesn't sneak up on me. And if you see a small red dot paint me, shout out. That means he's drawing a bead on me."

"Yer own father would kill ye?" Benji asked, his voice ending in a shocked squeak.

"I wouldn't put anything past that beast. I haven't done anything wrong but be born. To that superstitious son of a Viking, though, that's enough."

Benji scanned the verdant lakeshore as Mac trudged through the tall reeds and swamp grass, tuned in to the *beep, beeps* that were getting closer and closer together, an audible game of colder-warmer on the locator function of his phone.

The pings became a constant thrum as Mac zeroed in on his target. "Got 'em!" he shouted back just as his Benji noticed the red light cutting across the tall grass.

"Duck!" Benji screamed.

Thump! Thump! Thump! Three shots hit the trunk of the tree Mac had been standing beside, bark dust exploding and scattering in all directions.

Benji looked to where the *pop-pop-pops* had come from but couldn't see the shooter. It had to be Storm, though. Who else?

And then they both heard it. The *varoom-varoom-varoom* of a big-engined motorcycle, speeding away.

"Crap!" Mac huffed as he crawled out of the mire he had dove into.

"No, I'd say it was more like mud," Benji offered, sniffing the air. "Although if someone had been shootin' at me, I probably would have shat my pants."

Mac wrinkled his nose, too, then chuckled. "Nah. Just mud." He sobered up quickly. "What was I thinking? I should have known better."

"What do ye mean?"

"He threw away his glasses to draw me out. He had a plan and I walked right into it. And on top of everything else," he said, waving them in the air, "these are decoys."

"So, what's with those shades?" Benji asked. "Why are they so important?"

Mac turned them over, wiped them with the back of his hand, and squinted, inspecting them carefully. "Well, I'll be. Maybe not knock offs after all. Here, look," he said, pointing to the arm of the sunglasses.

"It looks like they're cracked maybe."

"Nope. I didn't see that when I was checking them out while in the mud, kicking myself – figuratively – for falling into his trap. I thought these were dollar store sunglasses. I mean, I thought they were just generic sunglasses, not smartglasses."

"*Smart* glasses? What? Do they have glasses that talk to you in yer time?" Benji asked with a chuckle that suddenly turned serious. "Glasses that talk to ye? Really?"

"More than just talk to you. Grandpa." Mac held the glasses in the air, looking through the lenses. "Too much mud. I need to get back to your place and clean these up. Damn! Sorry about bringing this filth into your rig. I guess I could ride in my skivvies – if I was wearing any."

"Dinna fash," Benji said.

Mac stared at him, confused.

Seeing the look, Benji started again. "That means, 'Don't worry.' I always keep a spare set of clothes in the van fer Janie and me, jest in case. I've needed them once or twice. The same ones are in there fer Janie. She's not as messy."

Back at the van, Mac quickly stripped and stepped into Benji's work coveralls. "Thanks. Hand me that bottle of water, would you?"

Benji handed it to him, then pulled a clean shop rag out of the console. "This might help."

"Any other surprises you keep hidden in this beast of yours?"

"Lots, but I dinna think we have time to run them down. Any other fancy tricks on that genius phone of yers?"

Mac snorted at the pun about his smartphone. "Yeah, more tricks than I have time to run through. One thing it doesn't have is a weapon." He looked up and raised an eyebrow.

Benji answered the tacit question. "I dinna carry a gun or a bow, but I always have a knife of some sort on my person plus one in the glovebox."

"What's a glovebox?"

Benji smacked the one on the dash and it popped open. He rummaged through it, found the spare Leatherman, and handed it to Mac. "Here, have a genius knife to go with yer genius phone."

Mac opened it up, tool by tool, his smile growing with each instrument revealed. "Is this mine?"

"If ye want it, it's yers. Jest don't try to take it through airport security or they'll seize it. It does have a blade and is considered a weapon."

He turned it over a couple of times. "What? No taser?"

"If a man's close enough to use a knife, I dinna think he needs a taser."

"True. Let's get out of here. Would you drive while I check these out? Oh, and don't take a direct route. He's probably watching where we're going."

"He might be, but I did hear the bike go quite a ways up the road. And I never heard it shut off."

"That's true. By the way, do you happen to have a fishing kit in here?"

"Never leave home without it." Benji opened the hidden compartment behind the front seat and pulled out a plastic box filled with fishing tackle. "Do ye need the rod, too? It's in the back."

"Nope. All I need are the lead sinkers."

Benji grabbed the ones from the box and handed them to Mac. "Buildin' a shield?"

"Smart man," Mac said.

"Smart enough," Benji replied. He handed him a can of Sterno and a small tin camp drinking cup from the same cubby the box had been in. "I'll try not to hit any bumps so ye dinna burn yerself. Ye did plan on meltin' it down, aye?"

"Actually, I was going to see if I could hammer the pieces flat, but I like your idea better. I think I'll ride back here on the floor, just in case. I don't want hot lead in my lap." Mac looked around nervously. "Let's get out of here. I hate this time of day."

"The goblin hour," Benji said. "Or something like that."

"Yeah, something like that…"

***

Within minutes, Mac had constructed a shield over the arm of the sunglasses where the mini computer's transmitter was, using the screwdriver of the Leatherman as a mold so he didn't have to heat up and possibly damage the electronics in the earpiece.

"At least he can't track us now," Mac said. His stomach roared.

"Unless he has good ears and hears yer waim." Benji chuckled nervously. "Is he really a murderer?"

"I don't know. If you were sure someone was going to kill you, wouldn't you try to get rid of him first, before he could get to you?"

"No," Benji said, then paused and added, "I'd try to talk him out of it." When Mac snorted his disagreement, he elaborated. "If I jest ran away, I'd always be lookin' behind my back. Afraid like ye were today."

"I wasn't afraid," Mac began, then realized he sounded like a liar or an idiot. "I was being cautious. I have to be. Shoot! Mom brought me up to always check my surroundings, never to trust anyone, always have an escape route planned."

"Ye must have had a miserable childhood, bein' scared like that."

"I wasn't scared. Just cautious." His stomach grumbled again. "I'll be glad to get back to your house and the *coq au vin*."

"Aye, but I dinna think that's why yer stomach is makin' so much noise."

"Huh? What else could it be?"

"Every time ye've said somethin' that wasn't quite the truth, yer waim complained. 'At least he canna track us' and 'I wasna afraid.' I think both of those statements werena quite the whole truth."

"I guess you're right," Mac agreed. He waited to see if his stomach would grumble again. Nope. "He might have a DNA tracker. I don't know. It was new technology, just in the planning stage, when I left. However, if Storm can slip forwards twenty years or more, he could have brought back something like that with him."

"And since ye share the same DNA, he can sniff ye out like a dog?"

"Yeah. Maybe. And there isn't anything I can do to hide it... Oh, crap..."

"What?" Benji asked. When Mac didn't respond, Benji said, "Ye canna be saying, 'Oh, crap,' without givin' me a reason why? Are Janie or the girls in trouble?"

"No," Mac said then sighed deeply. "But Julianna's son is. We share the same paternal DNA."

***

"We held off as long as we could," Julianna said.

"But we were all famished and if the chicken had stayed in that sauce any longer, it would have been tough as leather," Mali added.

"So, I rescued a couple of big helpings for you two and set them in the refrigerator." Jane looked back at Daisy and grinned. "The icebox," she amended and watched Daisy sigh in understanding.

"I'll eat later," Mac said. "I have to get this done and I'm really not that hungry." His stomach grumbled. He looked at Benji, scowled, then amended his last remark. "I'm famished, but if I don't check these out right away, my upload window might disappear." He waited for the belly growl but it was silent. He nodded to Benji. "This shouldn't take too long – maybe fifteen minutes or so."

"Is there anythin' I can do to help?"

"Nope," Mac said. "Savin' my hide was enough."

"Saving your hide?" Daisy squeaked, then put a hand over her mouth, blushing at her impertinence.

Mac smiled. "You didn't think I dove into the mud just to play leapfrog, did you?" he asked, wiping a muddy smear from his cheek. "I was in a bit of peril for a minute or two. All is fine now, though." *Grumble, grumble.* Mac sighed and added, "The sooner I get this taken care of," shaking the smartglasses, "the sooner we can all relax."

"Julianna, if you would do the honors of reheating dinner for these gentlemen," Silas said, "I'd like to watch what Mac's up to with those fancy specs. I read about a prototype for something like them. Those had a heads-up display that projected onto the lenses. They also had discreet little speakers over the ears. I'm itching to see how these are constructed."

"No problem. Reheating food is one of my secret talents. Creating meals from scratch, not so much," she said, stepping next to him. She leaned over and kissed him on the temple, then patted him on the shoulder.

Mac choked on a snicker of a laugh, seeing the disparity in their heights. She looked over at him, one eyebrow raised. "Your brother makes that same laugh when I lean down to give him a kiss goodbye," she said coolly, then eyed him up and down. "So far, that's the only similarity I've seen between you two."

"I...I meant no disrespect," Mac sputtered. "It's just I'm the one who's usually bending down to...to..." He quit trying to explain himself and shook his head, grimacing.

Julianna pursed her lips and nodded, still steaming from the dig about her height but willing to let her nephew slide on this one.

"I'm sorry. Truly," Mac said, hoping to quickly clean up his messy *faux pas.* "And I do want to know about my brother, but I have to take care of these," he shook the glasses again, "light speed." Still keeping track of Daisy out of the corner of his eye, he saw her frown of confusion at his explanation. "I have to see to these as fast as I can."

Julianna sighed. *Yes, he was definitely her adopted son's brother. They both tried to make sure no hard feelings lingered.* "Go see what secrets are hiding in those glasses...nephew."

"Full report to follow...Auntie."

Mac's words of farewell were to Julianna, but his eyes were on Daisy. He grinned and nodded to her, making sure she knew he'd be back. She wasn't looking directly at him, but by the smile he received in reply, he knew she was curious about him, too.

Mac followed Silas into the recreation room. "So, tell me, nephew," the older gentleman said, trying to bring Mac down from the clouds of fantasy romance to the hard science of circuits and wireless data streams, "how do you access the information in those? Do you need any special tools?"

Mac reached up and adjusted the decorative lamp in the ceiling above the bar to shine on the dark polished counter, then sat down on a barstool. "You just have to be clever," he said, his somber face brightening into a mischievous smirk. "And have the best data decryption programs ever created."

"If you need more light, my not-as-smart-as-yours phone has a flashlight function." Silas held it up, ready to hit the icon.

"Hmm...maybe..." Mac mused, squinting as he peered into the arm of the frames.

"I think I have this. Allow me," Silas said, stepping behind the bar.

Mac moved back and Silas snapped a picture. "Better than a microscope," Silas said. He opened the image on his phone, then pinched with thumb and forefinger to enlarge the image. He set it in front of Mac like a rare jewel.

"How quaint. I forgot about that function. Simple yet amazingly effective."

Laughter from the kitchen seeped into the den. Mac sat up straight, his eyes narrowed in concentration, then his hint of a smile grew into a wide grin when he realized who the sweet and timid laugh belonged to.

Silas saw it. "Yes, I'd say that was your Daisy."

"My Daisy?" Mac asked.

"Well, she certainly isn't mine or Benji's. We've both been claimed. By her sidelong glances at you and deep sighs, I'd say she's set her cap for you, whether she thinks she's worthy or not."

"She's worthy of anyone, but what do you mean 'set her cap'?" Mac asked.

"That phrase is older than I am by at least three generations, so she'd probably recognize it. It means she's waiting for you and only you."

Mac snorted in a combination of embarrassment and pride. "If so, it's because I'm the only single-ish man she's met in this century." He suddenly paled and tried to shake off his uneasiness about the prophecy. One version of it alluded to its onset in less than a week. "I have to concentrate."

Mac swiped a long finger across the screen of his own device, his face blank, then frowning. A slight smile began, then a flurry of taps and slides later, his mood erupted into pure joy. "Eureka!" he exclaimed. He looked at Silas. "That means…"

"I have found it," Silas said. "That word's attributed to Archimedes." He paused and added with a chuckle, "And he's older than my great-great-grandfather!"

"Yeah, well, greatness is timeless. Let's hope that Storm's fear is compromising his judgment." Mac's eyes widened and he scowled in uncertainty. "And that I didn't just start a countdown."

Chapter 17

"Is anyone hungry?" Jane asked from the doorway, ushering Daisy in with a tray of food. She looked from Mac to Silas and back again. "What's wrong?"

"Nothing," Mac said. *Grumble, grumble.* He huffed at his biological lie detector and changed his answer. "I don't know. I guess fatigue, hunger, and fear are getting to me. Here's hoping a hearty dish of calories will clear my head and steady my resolve."

"All right, then. I'll leave you two alone," Jane said and turned to leave.

Mac looked down at his hands. He had used a rag to wipe most of the mud and grime from them, but they certainly weren't clean enough to eat with.

"Oh, I brought a damp cloth for you...Mac," Daisy said, stumbling on his name, bowing her head. Suddenly, emboldened by Jane's final directions before entering the room, her chin popped up and she looked Silas in the eye. "And your fiancée said she'd tend to your *needs*," she said with the same emphasis her new friend had used.

Silas grinned at the word 'needs.' It was their secret word for passion. Evidently, Julianna was sending coded messages to him through an innocent. "My needs?" he asked, then chuckled. "Ah, yes. I'll let her feed me dessert. She likes doing that, you know. You two enjoy your repast," he said to Mac.

Daisy looked from Silas to Mac and back again, confused and wide-eyed.

"He means enjoy dinner," Mac said, scowling at Silas.

Silas's cheeks reddened. "Sorry. Me and my damned Yankee talk. I'm from Massachusetts, you know."

Daisy shook her head slowly. "No, I didn't know, but that's good to hear," her grimace of uncertainty now a sweet smile of appreciation. "A blessed Yankee," she added under her breath.

Mac noticed the hand towel and finger bowl beside the covered dish of food. "I don't think that's big enough for these," he said, holding up his hands. "I'll just use the sink."

He turned on the faucet in the bar sink, ran his hands under the water, and pumped the soap dispenser with his wrist. He lathered up, singing 'Happy Birthday to You,' softly as he scrubbed, then looked up at Daisy. "Oh, it's just a song my mother taught me to sing so I'd wash my hands long enough."

She didn't say a word but nodded that she'd heard, her face empty of emotion.

He could tell she understood the words but not the concept. "We've learned that washing hands with soap," he nodded to the white crane-billed apparatus, "helps us stay healthy. We don't get sick so often." He feigned a cough into his elbow then looked up and smiled at her. "Healthy and happy. Come here. I'll bet you've never seen liquid soap before, have you?"

She shook her head, then set down the tray on the table and walked toward him, head bowed, her steps apprehensive.

"Here, let me show you," he said, reaching out.

She held out one hand and let him lead her to the front of the basin. He nudged the single faucet handle with the back of his wrist, tested the temperature again, then held her hand in his under the flow. "Give me the other one, too," he said softly.

What had started as a lesson in twenty-first-century hygiene had suddenly become a romantic first contact. He used his free hand to pump the soap onto his fingers then massaged it into her long fingers and palms, his loins warming at the feel of her flesh slick and smooth, firm and yielding, under his touch. He gasped as he realized he was becoming aroused, then coughed to try and mask his obvious sigh.

"It feels nice," she said softly, looking up at him.

His eyes met hers. "It feels nicer washing someone else's hands. I mean, it's not the same when they're just your own. The feel of someone else's body under yours... I mean..."

Mac looked away, his face suddenly warm. He knew he had to be blushing. He hadn't done that in years. Or felt a connection to anyone who might bring it on since he was a sophomore in high school. He spotted the food tray on the table. "Here, let's rinse off completely then dry with a paper towel. You can catch someone else's cooties by using the same towel, too. No reason to wash if you're going to spread germs right away with one of those."

Daisy frowned in confusion.

"Don't worry about what I just said," Mac explained, shaking his head. "Sorry, I'm babbling. I guess I'm hungrier than I thought. Just know that it's better to air dry your hands or use one of these paper towels. I'm sure I'd be confused with words from your time. That's many yesterdays ago for me. I know words change all the time now."

Daisy smiled wide and nodded. *Yes, he is a gentleman even if a bit daft. Kind, big, strong, helpful, but also vulnerable and honest. I like him a lot!*

Mac pointed to the chair at the table. "Would you sit with me?" he asked. "I don't often have company to share a meal with."

Mac pulled her chair out, not wanting to take the chance he'd get a 'No, thank you' reply. He sat opposite her and set the napkin on his lap. When he looked up, he noticed her staring at him. "What's wrong? Do I have mud on my face?" he joked.

She nodded and said, "Just a little bit."

He started to reach up, then brought his hand back and said, "Would you do the honors?"

She picked up the small cloth next to the finger bowl, then leaned forward and dabbed at the smear on his cheek and the side of his nose. She pulled away and smiled, refolding the hand towel with the soiled side in.

"I take it I don't look like a pig now," he said.

"You never looked like a pig," she replied and pulled her chin to her chest, cheeks burning with a blush.

Changing the subject, he asked, "Did you get enough to eat? I have plenty here."

"Yes, I did. It was very good."

Mac used his knife to nudge some of the meat away from the thigh bone, then cut off a piece and sampled it. "Oh, man! This is the bomb!"

Daisy's shoulders hunched up to her ears and she looked around the room, panicked.

"What's wrong?"

"Bomb?" she squeaked, slipping down in her seat as if ready to hide under the table.

"Bomb?" he repeated. "Oh, bomb! That just means it's fantastic, great, stupendous. I'm sorry. I didn't mean to frighten you. I'm not familiar with eighteenth-century vernacular." He saw her eyes widen at the 'v' word. "Sorry. I'll just shut up and eat."

"No, it's all right. I have to learn how people talk now." Daisy's eyes shifted towards the hall she had come in from. The chatter and

103

laughter of the others softened the ambiance of the room even more than the soft late afternoon light through the windows.

"What?" he asked.

"Jane told me she wasn't going to send me back. I hope she doesn't change her mind."

"Why would she? I mean, you're free here. Did you want to go back? I'm sorry. I don't think anyone asked you, did they? Is that what you want? Do you have family? Children?" Mac asked, then added pensively, "A husband?"

She snorted, indignant. "A slave with a husband? No, I don't have a 'man,' and I don't have children." She giggled then brought her hand up in front of her mouth, trying to cover her slip of emotion.

"What's so funny about not having children?"

She giggled again, looked him in the eyes, then shifted her focus away and said, "I run too fast."

A sudden laugh escaped and Mac brought up his hand to keep from sputtering his dinner. He swallowed a gulp of iced tea and saluted her with the glass. "Ditto!"

"Ditto?"

He swallowed hard. "I mean, same here. No kids. I run fast, too."

She laughed freely, so he did, too. He suddenly took another bite of the chicken, feeling another blush rise on his face.

"I wouldn't run from you, though," she said softly.

Her head was down as she spoke, her words so gentle and smooth, they felt like sheer fabric across his face. He looked up when he heard her, making sure they weren't his own thoughts echoing in his head.

"How's it going in here?" Benji asked, stepping into the quiet room with a father's bold bravado. "Just making sure you two aren't up to any mischief."

"Dad!" Mali scolded, rushing up to put her hand on Benji's shoulder and pull him back. "You used to do that to me. It embarrassed the hell out of me."

"Ah, so it worked, aye? I mean, if ye were up to the devil's work and I came in and scared the hell out of you..." His eyes shone in merriment. "Dinna fash. Those two are both adults. I jest wanted to give wee Daisy a chance to leave if my grandson was bothering her."

"He's not bothering me," Daisy said softly, her face looking down at the table. She looked up and repeated herself, "He's not bothering me."

"And she's not bothering me, either," Mac said, then chuckled. "And didn't you say there was dessert tonight?"

"No, I didn't, but yes, there is," Benji said. "Daisy, if ye'd be so kind as to help Janie in the kitchen…" He stepped back to give her room.

As soon as she was gone, Mali escorting her, Mac stood up from the table and took two sharp strides to stand nose-to-nose with Benji. "What was that all about?"

"Yer movin' too fast," Benji said. "Remember, I have experience with this and ye dinna."

"I don't care two fat rat's tails if you do. Daisy isn't Jane and you're not me. And if it makes any difference, Daisy is also more than a hundred years ahead of Granny." Mac snorted, trying to calm down, then remembered something. "And do you know what a telegraph is?"

"See, yer not as bright as ye thought ye were. A telegraph is sort of an early form of email. Folks sent messages over a wire, usin' long and short electric tones of a sort to represent letters. Dots and dashes in certain combinations would be used to spell out words. They sent the signals over wires – like telephone wires."

"Since when did telephones have wires?" Mac asked.

Benji rolled his eyes. "I dinna ken who taught ye history, but that's not what I came in here to talk to ye about."

"Oh, so you didn't just come in here to make sure we weren't playing hide the sausage?"

"What? Now that's crude, young man…"

Mac shook his head, embarrassed. "Yes, it is. I'm sorry. It's just that we were making a connection. I wasn't sure if anyone asked her if she wanted to stay here. Just for the record, she doesn't have children or a man back in her time. I didn't know slaves couldn't marry. Jeez, how horrible. I mean…" Mac snorted in derision. "Sorry. So, what was it you wanted to talk to me about?"

"The coins. I guess there's the possibility she took the whole bag and hid it. At least, that's what Silas seems to think."

"Where is he?" Mac asked. "And did he take…" He saw the ice bucket Silas had stuck the sunglasses in as a joke. "No, I guess he didn't take them."

"Did ye find what ye needed with them?"

"I'm still running the decryption program. I got the file cloned but I have a clench there's something more to them than the program," Mac said and bit his bottom lip, musing.

"A clench?" Benji asked. "Now there's a term I've not heard of."

"A clench," Mac explained, his hand on his belly. "You know, when your belly or stomach or whatever you call it tightens up."

"Ah, a clench. That's a good one. Now that ye mention it, I have a clench someone could come sneaking in here to retrieve them. Since ye took off the lead sinkers, did ye do somethin' else so he canna track them?"

"Crap! No!" Mac popped up from the table and rushed to the ice bucket on the counter. He lifted the lid off and used the pair of ice tongs next to it to pick up the glasses, handling them as if they were wired to explode. He realized the lead sinker shield had not been replaced and grunted as he set them back into their hiding place. "Crap! Crap! Crap! What was I thinking?" he huffed as he set the lid back down.

"I'd say ye were thinkin' about the lass in the other room, or maybe jest that ye had to get the information downloaded or whatever it was ye were doing, in a hurry. Or maybe it was jest because ye were hungry…"

Mac chuckled. "You know, Grandpa, you can make up more excuses for my fouls than I can."

"If by fouls you mean messes, aye. I'm fairly adept at makin' excuses fer others. I try to take responsibility for my own screw ups, though."

"Ahem," Silas said, standing behind the two redheads. "It was me this time, not Mac. I'm a little leery of lead but have found that copper works just as well at blocking signals. That's a copper signal interference shield, disguised as an ice bucket. I take it with me when I travel for stashing phones, credit cards, or other items with microchips."

"Really…" Mac drawled, then looked at the old man with new appreciation. "That's pretty clever."

"Hide in plain sight," Silas said. "I've never had anyone rifle a room while we were gone and look in the ice bucket for valuables. Not that I'd leave any goods like those behind, but I have noticed signs of trespassing while…"

Woof, woof, woof! Grrr! Woof, woof, woof!

"What in the hell?" Benji asked, rushing to the French doors to look outside.

"It's Duchess," Silas said. "And I think she found a skunk." He tiptoed up for a better look and added. "The two-legged kind."

The sound of twigs snapping and leaves rustling in the azaleas, sweeping against each other in protest, were as good as a spotlight on the area of confrontation. A sharp mumbled curse in a foreign tongue bellowed out, answered with more loud grumblings from the huge Australian Shepherd mix dog. Suddenly, a loud and unnatural 'thud' – like a localized sonic boom – stilled the air. The dog and everything else silenced. Two blinks and a hiccup later, the faint whine of an electric motor pierced the air like a mosquito at midnight, followed by the crackle of tires on an unpaved roadbed.

"I'd say Storm's back," Mac said dryly.

Silas and Benji ran outside to investigate but Mac stayed in the den. He looked to the ice bucket but didn't move it. If Storm was searching for the sunglasses, he wouldn't expect them to be on the counter. Silas was right. Hide in plain sight. Instead, he looked in the cabinets under the bar, pulling out bottles and boxes until he found what he wanted: a near-empty container. He took the rest of the little packets of stevia sweetener from the carton and added them to the others in the decorative cup next to the coffee pot.

Now for the decoy. He had noticed the small library near the French doors when he first came in. It was stocked with shiny new books and magazines about babies and pregnancies along with a well-worn stack of romance novels. He picked up one with a handsome lovestruck couple on the cover – a redhaired man and a black woman. He grinned, noticing that the dogeared paperbacks seemed to get more attention than the informative materials. Ah, that's what he was hoping for. In the middle of the table was a small rectangular wicker basket with at least six pairs of reading glasses. "I don't think the lady of the house will mind if I borrow a pair." He rummaged through the lot, finding the ones closest in size to the ones Storm had tossed. He put them in the little green box, wrapped a couple of tissues around it, then placed it next to the stereo, mostly – but not completely – hidden. "Decoy."

***

"I guess it was a wise decision to keep the dog," Benji said.

"I don't think she likes Swedish meatballs," Silas said, smirking, trying to hold back a laugh at his own joke.

"Norwegian nutballs is more like it. Where's Mac? Maybe he knows what that big boom was."

"Your grandson's inside with the goods, making sure someone doesn't double back, I'm sure. He's young but seems to have some great instincts."

"Plus, some fancy tools," Benji added. "Although ye have a few yerself, I gather."

"Nah, I was just blessed with a healthy dose of common sense and practicality. That and I read a lot; self-taught, as it were." He looked up and saw four women, shoulder to shoulder, coming out of the house towards them.

"I take it the danger is over?" Jane asked.

"Fer the moment, maybe forever. It appears Mac's sire has figured out where we are. We need to find out what he wants and either give it to him or negotiate."

"Or neutralize him," Mac said. He cut his eyes back to the room he had just come from, letting it be known he had everything under control.

"Translate, please," Jane said.

"Yes, please," Mali added.

Julianna moved close to Silas and wrapped her arm around him. "Can we take this inside?" Silas asked, nodding with a scowl to Mac.

"Good idea," Mac replied. "There are too many bugs out here for me."

Jane and Benji led the way, Silas and Julianna behind them, leaving Mac with Daisy and his mother. "Shall we?" he asked, putting his arms out.

Daisy followed Mali's lead and threaded her arm through Mac's, tingles and goose pimples running up her arm and across her chest as she did so. She noticed Mali squeezing close to Mac then pulling away, so she did, too. A smile came to her face. She probably wasn't supposed to do that part – Mali was Mac's mother and that was probably the reason for the hug – but she'd claim ignorance and enjoy that warm, fuzzy sensation. She had learned long ago that it was better if people thought she was dumb.

But she wasn't.

Chapter 18

Grrr!

"Foul beast!" Storm snorted. He waved the poison-laced steak in front of the angry mixed-breed sheepdog, then threw it into the trees.

Duchess, still in guard dog mode, wasn't even tempted. At the stranger's quick movement, her low growl erupted into a loud raucous barking alert. She lunged forward then took quick steps back, keeping the intruder away from her new family.

"Blasted vegetarian," Storm huffed. "Time for Plan B."

His eyes on the noisy hound, Storm reached into his shoulder bag and found what he was after. He quickly stuck the bionic ear protectors in place, then glanced down and made sure the shocker was set to stun. Tossing it a few feet over her head, he called, "Catch, bitch!"

KABOOM!

As if hit by a car, Duchess was knocked to the ground. Stilled and unresponsive, she couldn't so much as lift a paw. She lay where she dropped, her eyes following the man in white as he opened his bag and took out a long knife.

Storm glanced at his pale silk slacks and huffed. These were the last ones he had left. Rather than gut the dog – his first inclination – he bent down and sliced through her leather neckwear, a belt improvised as a collar and leash contraption, then stepped back and snorted. "That'll teach you to mess with the son of Loki." He took out his marker, scribbled a quick ransom note on the inside of the belt, then tossed it toward the front door.

As he stepped away, Duchess curled her lip. She huffed a weak growl but was otherwise paralyzed.

"On second thought," Storm said. He looked at the house, then turned back quickly. "I have a better idea. You really are coming with me, mutt." He squatted down and hoisted her like a load of dirty laundry, holding her as far away from his body as he could without stumbling in the dark. "That's all I need is for you to snap out of it early and let them know where I am."

***

"That was a shocker," Mac said without preamble, coming outside via the side door to join the other six. "It won't hurt you unless it hits you. It's used to disperse mobs of people or wild critters."

"I'd say it was pretty effective," Benji said, finger wiggling in his ear as if he could shake his sense of hearing back into alignment. "Especially if it was meant to prevent those involved from communicatin' with each other. It seems to suck the noise right out of the air."

"And it also neutralizes electronics if they're close enough." Mac patted his chest, searching for his phone. He gasped in exaggerated panic but grinned broadly. "I guess I'm screwed there."

Silas opened his mouth, ready to comment, but was stilled by Mac's quick scowl and silent admonition, head shaking back and forth minimally. He cupped his hand to his ear and Mac nodded in agreement. *Watch what you say – he might be listening.*

"Well, since we're back to square one, everyone, how about a game of darts?" Benji suggested.

"Might as well," Mac said brightly but with a grimace. *What are you up to, Grandpa?*

"To the game room!"

Everyone filed back into the den Mac and Silas had been in earlier, the 'ice bucket' still on the counter. Benji reached onto a shelf and put in a CD of classic disco music, turning the volume up to barely tolerable.

Daisy bolted at the sudden noise and clung to Jane.

"Don't worry. You'll get used to it," she said. "They've figured out how to gather sounds and stick them onto a little plate...or make it even smaller still. Now that bad man who attacked us with his car can't listen to us. Come on. Let's find out what our men have to say."

Silas whispered into Julianna's ear, pointing to the dartboard on the wall.

"Got it," she told him. "Come on, Mali," she said loudly. "I'll bet washing dishes for a week that I can beat you three out of five games."

Mali watched her sister's face and saw they were to be the ambient noise distraction. "In your dreams!" she hollered. "Big sisters rule! Come on, Daisy. Let's see if you can best her, too."

The chatter continued, the two older women showing Daisy how to play, pointing out that the closer to the center, the more valuable the shot. In matriarch mode, Jane flitted between the two groups, pacing between the dart-throwing ladies and the men who were deep in conversation about their options.

"Janie, did Daisy say anythin' to you about more coins?" Benji asked on her next trip back.

"She gave me that one coin when I first met her. She didn't say anything that led me to believe she had more, though. She said she found it in the dirt. Boss Man chased her to get it and the next thing she knew, she was here. Now."

Jane looked up and saw all three men's faces just inches from hers, listening intently, trying to drown out the Bee Gees in the background. She chuckled at the words of the song. "Yes, I think she was just stayin' alive."

Mac chewed a grin, not wanting to give in but finding it hard not to. He looked over at Daisy, laughing with his aunt and mother, already fitting into her new family dynamics. "Do you think she'd lie to us?"

"No!" Jane said sharply. "I don't think it's in her." She paused, reflecting on her own life as a slave. Lying would get a person flogged...if he or she was lucky. The loss of an ear or branding on the face if not. "No, she wouldn't lie."

"But she wouldn't volunteer everything she knew, either," Silas said. "No offense, but that's part of Survival 101. Share just enough to keep you safe and whole."

Jane sighed but didn't say anything, then nodded.

"My mother said she's the one who took the coins," Mac said. "It doesn't matter where she got them, just that she got them away from him. For all we know, he has an army of Lokis just waiting to create the ultimate chaos," he added with a nod to Benji, acknowledging his grandfather's earlier analogy. "Maybe we ought to talk to Mom and Daisy together."

"Or separately and see if their stories jive," Silas said, then looked at the others. "No offense, but we're talking about the elephant in the room. Everyone has a different take on what happened. What Mali saw as a wall, Daisy may have seen as a rope."

"Huh?" Mac asked.

"The parable of three blind men and the elephant. Each one felt a different part. The body was like a wall, the tail like a rope..." Benji said, then shook his head. "Everyone's perception is different."

"I'll take that as fact. Time's running out, though. Silas, you're pretty good at reading body language; I'd like your help, please."

Silas rubbed his hands together diabolically. "Ah, I love a challenge."

"Be nice," Benji said. "Dinna be scarin' the lass. From what I've seen of Mali, she can handle anyone. Daisy, however..." he shook his head, not verbalizing the rest of his remark. *Is as naïve as a babe and probably jest as helpless.*

"I'll get her," Silas volunteered. He walked over to the dartboard, watching the game for a few throws.

"Care to take me on?" Julianna asked him, not even trying to suppress the twinkle in her eye.

Even though the music was still loud, Daisy had heard the remark and seen the unspoken communication. She cast her eyes down bashfully but not before she had looked to see Mac's reaction. He grinned then immediately turned his head away from the flirting pair, a slight blush rising on his neck.

"Well, Mac?" Mali asked. "Care to join us? I'll bet Daisy can already best you."

Mac's neck reddened up to his forehead. "No. We need to talk first. You, me, and Silas. Follow me to the john."

All the bathrooms in the custom-built house were large. Benji had designed them oversize specifically for pregnant women. Still, fitting three people into one room – two very tall people and one above average – made for close quarters. Mac flipped on the fan. "I don't think he can hear us in here, but just in case... Mom, where – and when – did you hide Storm's coins. And how many were there?"

"They were hidden just across the water from our place. When was May of 1864. I'm not sure about the exact date."

"Grandpa's new place here in North Carolina? You mean, pretty much near the trees you and Julianna were hiding in when we got here?" Mac asked.

"We weren't hiding, but yes. I couldn't see the exact spot where they were buried and didn't have a locator at the time, either. I didn't care. I just wanted them out of his hands. I took one coin out for me, then buried the bag. I didn't think I'd dropped one, but I guess it's possible."

"So, you still have the coin you came in on?"

"Well, not exactly," Mali said, her head bowed so he didn't see her face.

Mac looked at the top of her head, the only part visible, then over to Silas. He shrugged then shook his head.

"Mother," Mac said, using the no-nonsense voice he used with ruffians, "either you have it or you don't. It's a simple yes or no answer."

"Well, I did have it. I even showed it to Julianna when we were up in the tree. I didn't *do* anything with it, but I don't have it now."

"Was it in your pocket, on a pendant…" Mac saw her eyes brighten at the last word. "So, maybe the chain broke somewhere between the old manse and here?"

"It must have. I never took it off. I didn't flash it around, either. It was always tucked inside my shirt. Oh, Lord. I hope Storm didn't pick it up. He didn't have one. He…um…put all his eggs in one basket and I stole the basket."

"Except for the token you kept." Mac huffed and turned away. He caught movement out the bathroom window. "Hold that thought. Or think of where you were when it might have fallen off. I'll be right back."

Mac sneaked outside and watched the bushes rustle. Something or someone was heading toward the house. He rushed hunched over like a large feral animal to the end of the hedge, waiting at the patio. Just as the shuffling reached the concrete, he stood up and stepped into the path of the interloper. "What are you doo…"

"Eek!" Daisy screamed and squatted to the ground, hands over her head, knees to her chin and chest.

"Geez, woman!" he exclaimed. "I thought you were Storm, sneaking back here to cause more trouble."

Still buried in her knees, her head shook back and forth, no sound other than a whispered whimpering of, "Don't beat me."

"What? No, no. It's me who's sorry. I didn't mean to terrorize you. I mean, I wouldn't have shouted if I'd known it was you. What are you doing out here?"

Still cowering, Daisy turned her head, focusing on his chin rather than his eyes. "Look…looking for the dog. Looking for Duchess. She's gone."

"Here, get up," Mac said, reaching his hand out to her. "You didn't do anything wrong. Just the opposite. We should have checked on her stat."

Daisy stared at his hand. Her gut instinct was to shy away from it, but it was open and inviting, not clenched into a fist or poised to slap. And it was Mac's.

She put her hand in his and felt a surge of warmth race up her arm. Like the taste of a spoonful of molasses, sweet tingles fluttered in her belly. He brought her hand toward him, not letting go, but not restraining either. Comforting. Assuring.

What have you got yourself into now, Mac. Let go now! If your grandpa doesn't thwack you for making a pass at her, life sure will. You can't be traipsing through time with a woman who doesn't even know what a solar panel is, much less electricity.

"The dog," Daisy whispered, bringing Mac out of his introspection. "I didn't think she'd run away."

Mac patted her hand then let it go. "I'll find her." He pulled out his genius phone and tapped and swiped across the screen.

Ping! Ping! Ping!

He looked toward the door twenty feet away. "She should be right there. Come on," he said, his hand gentle on her shoulder.

Daisy looked up, curious about the noise but more intrigued by the familiar touch that had her tiptoeing up into it rather than shirking away.

Mac explained. "I put my belt on her as a collar. It has a tracker in it."

Her eyes wide in confusion, he showed her the image on his phone. A series of red circles raced out like ripples from a stone thrown in a lake at sunset. "The middle is where it is, right?" she asked.

"Yes, ma'am," he said brightly, realizing he still had his hand on her and she wasn't flinching. Instead, she was walking with him, two mismatched bodies moving as one toward the sound.

There it was, a tangle of leather that had been tossed or dropped three feet from the door, almost in the herb garden. He picked it up and brought it toward the porch light. "Coins 4 dog," he read. "Not very original," he added. "Same ransom note. I'll bet he doesn't even have her."

"Then where is she?" Daisy asked.

"Crap. Sorry. Maybe you're right. If she was out here – and we both know by her barking that she was – then the shocker could have stunned her enough that he could have taken her. Damn!" He turned to her. "Sorry again. Come on. Let's go inside."

Daisy gasped slightly as he took his hand from her shoulder to hold open the door, then sighed as she felt its warmth return once they were inside. Was he claiming her as a friend or just making sure she didn't run away? Jane had assured her she was free. A gentleman wouldn't return his touch to a woman unless he was fond of her. She'd seen it many times when Mistress O'Leary had gentlemen callers. She reached up and lay her hand on his and left it there, just as her mistress had done to the man she had chosen. Mac may speak words that were strange to her, but hopefully the language of bodies was the same whether it was yesterday, today, or tomorrow.

Chapter 19

"Hey, everyone," Mac announced.

Benji turned down the music and looked up, waiting.

"Duchess is missing. I found this." He held up the belt, showing the words written in black marker.

"Coins for dog," Silas read. "Not very original." He looked at Julianna. "How did he get your scarf this afternoon anyhow?"

"It was in the car," she said. "He must have seen me take it off when I left for the trees. He didn't try to kidnap me or even interact with me on level one. Shoot! I knew him by Mali's description, but the first time I ever saw him was when we drove him and his beat-up Camaro off the road!"

"Intimidation, remember?" Mali said. "He's a bully. Whether he really has the dog or not, he's trying to draw us out, so we fight on his ground."

"But Duchess," Jane protested. "We have to get her back."

Mali shook her head. "He doesn't like messes. He's positively obsessed with image. He wouldn't want so much as a dog hair on him much less chance a blood splatter from shooting her or..."

Jane's hand went to her mouth suddenly.

"Sorry, Mom," Mali said.

Swallowing the acrid bile, Jane shook her head. "I'll be all right." She looked at Mac. "Can you track her with that fancy tool of yours?"

Mac's glower brightened into a wide grin. "Oh, yeah..." He nodded at Mali and held up his genius phone as if it held all the answers to the world's problems. He twisted it back and forth, showing it off. "Their hot little feet will show up brilliantly on this! Storm forgot – or didn't know – he'd have someone on his tail with the most advanced technology still in development."

Julianna stepped closer and peered at the device. "So, did you create this?"

"I modified an existing pocket computer with a few – dozen – features. Just think of it as a modern-day Leatherman tool. Everything you'll need in one little package...except a knife." He tapped the screen then held it up like a scanner, inspecting the area, focusing on where the shocker had been the loudest.

"Ah, there they were. See?" Mac showed the image with scatters of red lines to everyone. "Where the color is the brightest is where the most activity took place." He waved his hand over the screen, enlarging the image so he could focus on the details in that spot. "I can't be sure, but I'd say he picked her up and carried her away. At least, her tracks disappear and his are a brighter, a deeper hue. And they lead in that direction."

"That's where that odd whining noise came from," Jane said. She saw Mac staring at her. "Hey, as your grandfather told you, I have good hearing."

"Electric vehicle," Mali said. "He doesn't care for the stink of internal combustion machines. Unless it's a muscle automobile like that Camaro."

"Muscle car," Benji corrected.

"Then why was he so intent on causing the Valdez spill?" Julianna asked.

"Chaos, unrest, the upheaval of governments – conflicts of any kind," Mali said.

"Why?" Benji asked. When everyone looked at him, dumbfounded and wide-eyed, he explained himself. "If we ken why, we might be able to figure where he's headed, right?"

"Why is like the fascination people have with fire," Mac said. "It dances high and colorful – an unpredictable form without patterns. Fire is destructive but it also mesmerizes and transfixes us. The bigger the flames and the more diverse the ingredients consumed, the more colorful the display. He watches the confusion of the world in the same way. It's simply entertainment to him. Right, Mom?"

Mali shrugged one shoulder, embarrassed that she had ever been a part of his diversions.

"So, do ye have an idea where he'll be headed next? Maybe we can stop him."

"He has a fan base in 2018, Da," Mali said. "He's promised the coins to them in exchange for their loyalty. After they do his bidding, they can go wherever they want. Or so he says. I'm sure he'll figure a way to keep them on a short leash."

"Speaking of leashes," Jane said. "Can we discuss his great plans later and concentrate on finding Duchess. Please."

Daisy moved closer to Mac and lay her hand on his arm. "Yes, please?" she asked, coffee-dark eyes blinking back the sparkle of tears.

He gave her a quick hug for reassurance, then felt her snuggle into him, securing her position in his casual hold. He pulled her tight and kept her close. He spoke to the group but made sure Daisy knew his words were mostly for her. "It shouldn't be too much trouble to find them. Granny, would you come with Mali and me? Julianna, would you and Silas make sure no harm comes to Daisy and the rest?"

"What about me?" Benji asked.

"I thought that was understood. You're coming with us. We're getting the family hound back."

***

"Damned dark roads!" Storm hissed. "Where's a full moon when you need one."

Grr. Grr.

"Oh, coming out of it so soon?" he hissed at the dog. "Need a little extra dosing?" Storm held the silver orb the size of a ping pong ball between thumb and finger, waving it back and forth in front of her nose, making sure he didn't activate it and stun himself, too.

Duchess sighed in response and shut her eyes, exhausted.

Thunk! Thunk! Clink! Clank...clunk!

Sounds of machinery falling apart beneath him startled Storm. He tried to steer to the side of the road, but the vehicle was unresponsive. "Damn! I thought I just pulled the headlight module. Damned ancient jar of wingnuts and wires!"

Stopped in the middle of the road, Storm tried to open the door. "Blasted electronics!" He twisted his tall frame in the tiny driver's seat and kicked out the passenger window, scattering sheets of plasticized safety glass onto the roadway. A few more well-placed boot-heel blows and he had created a portal big enough for his tall body.

Scrambling out awkwardly, he looked around to make sure his embarrassing exit wasn't seen by anyone. He noticed the dog, still prone on the cargo deck in the rear. "You're on your own, sweetheart. Without lights, you and this plastic pile of rubbish will probably be obliterated by the next vehicle coming down the road." He patted his shirt pocket to make sure he still had his 'magic' marker with him, then began his trek, strutting as if any passing car would be privileged to pick him up.

***

118

The petite dark-haired woman watched Storm climb out through the shattered window of the Prius, as gangly as a one-armed monkey trying to get out of a toilet bowl. Ciara looked down at her phone again. The dog's vitals were still strong although the heart rate was slow – still groggy with a shocker hangover.

Hmph! I guess the dog did follow me here. And so did the slave. Even wearing that modern bright yellow dress, it was easy to recognize her as the young woman who dug up the coins for me. One of the drachmas must have come out of the bag. If she had been holding it while running through the trees, visualizing her freedom, she'd be free, alright. Free and a hundred and fifty years in the future.

You're lucky, woman. If you had stumbled upon anyone else, they would have thought you crazy. Julianna will make sure you're taken care of. That's what she does.

As soon as Storm was out of sight, Ciara came out of the ravine, smiling. She tapped the icon, then put her genius phone back in her hip pocket. Who knew that electronics jamming apps would work so well on cars built in 2010?

"Well, hello, Dog," Ciara said, opening the driver's door. She scooted the seat forward and pushed the start button. The motor hummed, ready to roll. She turned back and patted her former traveling companion on the head. "Do you want to go back and see your new family? I think they miss you."

* * *

"How does he expect us to give him the coins if we don't know how to contact him?" Benji asked Mac.

"Head this way," Mac said, navigating with his phone as Benji drove. "I don't know, but that's a good point."

"Kidnappers tend to leave a note of some sort telling where to leave the ransom," Benji said. "Or they tell ye in person. Did this Storm fellow say anything to ye?"

"No. Never," Mac said coldly.

"Even those idiots who kidnapped you and your sister had enough sense to do that," Jane said, referring to encounters from her husband's past. "I think Storm knows what we're doing. Or at least he knows where we are. He didn't have too much trouble finding us today. Does he have something like that?" she asked, nodding to Mac's device.

"Not that I know of. This is one of a kind. I developed it."

119

"Maybe he's part bloodhound and can sniff us out," Benji said, adding a nervous laugh.

"Shit!" Mac exclaimed. "Sorry, Granny. Shoot! You're both right. He tracked us to Bibb's house with the scarf he took from Julianna."

"But how could he do that?" Benji asked. "We took it with us."

Mac groaned, then pulled off the road. "Hold on. We're going back to the house."

He looked both ways then made a broad U-turn, speeding down the dark highway.

"Are ye gonna tell us?" Benji asked.

"Sorry. Sometimes I get so wound up in my head that I forget to speak. This," Mac held up the leather strap that had been used as a collar and a leash for Duchess. "What's different about this?"

"Other than the writing on the back, it looks no different than when ye used it as a belt."

"Exactly. The marker. He used the same marker on the scarf that we took back to the house. That's how he found out where we were. Right now, he knows we aren't there. Or at least I'm not there and probably the other big dude – you – who was driving earlier today."

"Ye mean he can track the ink on this belt?"

"Yup, Grandpa. He can."

"Well, shit!" Jane said. She saw both men stare at her. "Don't look at me! Watch the road and let's get back to my girls and Silas as fast as these wheels will take us. We have family to protect."

***

"Do you need anything, Daisy?" Julianna asked.

"No, thank you," she said. "I'm just tired."

"Well, you've had a long day. Go ahead and lie down. There's nothing to do but wait and worry. And since worry never helped anyone get anything done, it's just waiting time. You might as well do it while sleeping. Is it too cold in here for you? I know you're not used to air conditioning."

Julianna saw Daisy's eyes widen. "The artificial...manufactured...fake..." Each word she offered resulted in another look of confusion.

"The chilled breeze that comes out of the wall," Silas suggested.

Daisy smiled in appreciation and nodded.

Silas handed her the lap blanket from the back of a rocking chair. "Wrap up in this if you'd like. You can rest in your room or out here, your choice."

Taking the patchwork quilt and wrapping it around her shoulders, Daisy smiled but remained mute.

"Is that smile because you have your own room, or because you're getting a choice?" he asked.

"Both," she said. "If you're sure you don't need me…"

Julianna cuddled into Silas and sighed. "We have everything we need," she said.

"Good night, then," Daisy said, giving them an automatic bow as she backed out of the room. *My own room… with a real mattress and clean bedding, too!*

"She's so sweet," Julianna said. "I think she'll fit in well here."

"So, we're not staying?" Silas asked.

"Huh? Um, no, I didn't think we would," Julianna replied with a frown. "I was serious. I have everything I need with you. I think I've cleaned up any possible messes with my parents. Or at least explained my disappearance. Mali and I are cool, and now you're certain that time travel is real and I'm not a nut."

"Well, I don't know…" Silas drawled with a mischievous smile on his face.

"Which part is wrong?"

"I think you're still a nut, but you're *my* nut. My tall and elegant pecan, perfect as a main dish and delicious as a dessert." He nuzzled into her neck, then pulled back. "Are you sure you didn't do this just so I'd propose to you?"

She giggled at the sensation of his day-old whiskers on her neck. "You didn't have a chance."

"I'd have chased you to the beginning and end of time to get you to marry me," Silas said. "But, if you don't mind too much, I'd like to go back home. Home to 2010 and our families there."

"Our family. From the looks of it, we're going to be joined in more ways than one. Not only legally wed, but I don't doubt your granddaughter and my son will be giving us little ones within a year or two."

"I agree," Silas said. "I was tempted to look them up, but that's cheating. I don't want to interrupt the natural timeline. If something bad happened, I'd rather not know. Right now, I'm full of hope for their future. I don't want that dashed."

"Yes, I thought of snooping, too. As soon as all this is settled, I'd like to say farewell to my family here and go back. Oscar may not be my biological son, but he's as much a part of me as if built from one of my ribs."

"He's a part of your heart," Silas said, his hand slipping down from her neck to her left breast.

Her hand rested on his. "As are you," she whispered then slipped into his embrace.

"Are you sure we should be doing this?" Silas asked as her hand rubbed the front of his slacks, searching for the tab of his zipper.

"Only Daisy's here and who's she going to tell?" she giggled, then deftly unbuttoned his trousers. "Besides, I've seen the way she and Mac look at each other. If anything, she'll be jealous."

Silas moaned then yipped as she got a firm hold of him. "Ah, free at last, free at last…"

***

Daisy clutched the lap quilt around her shoulders and sat on the edge of the bed. She lifted herself up, then sat back down again, noticing the springiness. Curious, she knelt on the floor and looked under the bed. There weren't any ropes to hold the mattress off the ground, yet it was as bouncy as a twice-tightened bedframe. She stood up again and pulled the coverlet off the pillows and sniffed the sheets. A crisp clean smell, not even a hint of body odor. If she didn't know better – and she didn't – she'd bet that no one had slept on this bedding, or at least the linens. "Mine," she sighed, then kicked off her sandals, climbed into bed, and snuggled into the pillow. "I think I'm in heaven."

***

All silent, the van raced home, speed limits ignored. No one cared to talk or speculate about what could happen. Benji pulled off the highway and drove down the lane, smacking on the horn, startling Jane who had been nodding off.

"Who? What? Huh?" she babbled.

"If that fiendish villain is lurking about, I want him to know he willna be surprising my family."

"Why would he be coming back?" Jane asked.

122

"I think yer more tired than ye'd care to admit, wife. All he's been after is that bag of coins."

And the sunglasses and me, Mac thought. But I don't want to bring that up. As long as we neutralize him, those won't matter.

Daisy scrambled onto the floor at the noise, then rolled under the bed, reaching up for the small quilt to cuddle into.

Silas and Julianna grabbed for their clothes and rushed to make themselves decent. "I feel like a teenager," Silas huffed, tucking in his shirt, swiping away any possible lipstick from his face.

Julianna giggled, looking down at the disarray of his shirt and slacks. She tugged and pulled them into alignment and grinned.

"Better?" he asked.

She shrugged. "I doubt we'll fool anyone but that's okay. I'm sure Da will be happy that I've found someone respectable."

"Respectable enough to ask his permission to marry you," Silas said, planting a quick kiss.

"Do you think we ought to see why he honked?"

"Oh, shit!" Silas scrambled into his shoes. "You really do befuddle my brain, woman!"

Chapter 20

Benji burst through the door, Mac on his heels. "Is everyone all right?"

"Um, yeah, Da," Julianna said sheepishly, tucking a wayward tress behind her ear. "Thanks for the warning. What was all the honking about?"

"By the looks of yer clothes and hair, I'd say it was a good thing I did make a ruckus!" He huffed and shook his head. "I'm sorry. I was afraid someone would be lurking about and I meant to frighten him."

"Did you find the dog?" Silas asked.

Mac, standing behind Benji, frowned at Silas and mimed wiping his forehead. Silas mirrored the movement and looked down at his hand. He stuck it in his pocket and wiped off the dark smudge of eye makeup. "She didn't come back here," he said. "At least, I didn't hear her."

"So," Julianna tried again, "if you didn't find Duchess, why did you come back?"

Mac showed them the belt with one hand and held his finger to his lip with the other, admonishing them to be quiet. He pointed to the writing on the back of it, then fluttered his fingers in the air as if the words were flitting out the room.

"Ahh," Julianna and Silas gasped softly.

"Yup," Benji said boisterously but with a scowl, "I guess since we never had whatever coins this kidnapper wants, it doesn't make a difference. Easy come, easy go on the dog. I guess we'll just go to the pound and pick up a new one tomorrow."

"I suppose," Mac agreed, looking around the room. He mouthed, "Where's Daisy?"

Silas and Julianna pointed to the hall where her bedroom was and shrugged.

"I'll check on her," Mac said softly.

Benji started to protest, but Jane put a hand on his shoulder. "They're adults. He wouldn't press her into doing anything she didn't want, I'm sure."

He sighed and nodded in agreement. "Oh, aye, I remember… Still, we best be watching out fer that Storm fellow. I have the itchy, crawly feeling he's nearby."

"Thanks for the ride," Storm told the wrinkle-faced blonde sporting the perky bustline of a twenty-year-old. "It's a great car. I wouldn't mind having one like it."

"It's the only black '57 Corvette in the county," she said, rubbing his leg familiarly as he turned to get out. "Here's my card. Give me a jingle if you're ever in the Raleigh area. Or if you need a ride back."

Storm looked at the card and grinned: Carla Berndt, Investment Broker. "I won't forget you, for sure," he said, giving her a broad, toothy smile and a wink. *Not only her own money but access to her clients' funds, too.*

The perfectly painted, silicone'd, and coifed woman drove off without looking back. He wouldn't call her. She knew the type because she was the same. 'Use your friends and acquaintances wisely,' her father had told her. She reached into her pocket and took out the coin she had pinched from him with the friendly pat. She rubbed it between thumb and fingers, feeling its weight. Heavier than any American coin and lumpy, like an ancient one. It had a hole – no, two holes – in it. It didn't feel like gold. She'd have her jeweler appraise it next time she was in town. It should be worth at least the hassle of picking up a good-looking but obviously down-on-his-luck hitchhiker.

***

The next driveway was theirs. Just as Storm glanced up, the light flicked off in the garage. The van must have left, looking for him, and not too long ago. Had they all gone on the search? He fingered the last shocker. If any had stayed behind, he would take care of them.

The garage door had a clear panel in it: good for daylight illumination, but great for snooping to see if anyone was home.

Drat! Full – both the van and that monster of an old Cadillac are here. They've left and come back! Unless they're searching on foot, everyone is home.

Storm slinked around the house, looking up to make sure he wouldn't trip any motion-detector lights. Yes, they were everywhere. He sidled to the far end of the patio then doubled back and looked in each window as he passed. Was this some sort of dormitory? There had to be at least six bedrooms with double beds in each one. Must be fat kids.

The last room had movement. He waited patiently to make sure he hadn't imagined it. Yes, there was the little one – the runt of the four

125

women. She was crawling out from under the bed. He tested the knob on the patio door nearby. It was locked, but a quick tug and a well-placed punch, and *thwack,* the deadbolt pulled out of the door frame.

Storm inched his way in, ignoring the automatic light that popped on. Hopefully, no one was around to see it.

Terrified of the sudden bright light, Daisy crept back under the bed, hiding from the unknown. Suddenly, she saw shoes, lumpy footwear that looked like a colorful quilt made of stripes and arcs neatly arranged around the huge feet.

"Eek!" Despite her effort to remain still, the man's grasp startled a noise out of her. She tensed and turned to see who it was.

"It's all right," Mac said. "It's me. I was worried that you'd run away."

Her body softened with relief and a smile started on her face.

Then she saw 'him' and fainted into a limp mass of sundress and limbs.

Mac turned to see what had startled her but was cold-cocked before he could focus.

"So, that's what you look like up close," Storm said. "Hmm. Not bad looking if I do say so myself." He let Mac drop but held onto the girl. "Come on, sweetie. It's time to barter."
***

"What's takin' Mac so long?" Benji asked, not expecting an answer.

"Maybe he's asking Daisy to marry him," Mali teased. She looked at Silas and winked. "There seems to be a lot of that going around."

"You're just jealous because you haven't found anyone as cool as Silas," Julianna taunted, then hugged her fiancé.

"I haven't been looking because I've been trying to keep the world from falling apart!" Mali hissed. "You know what's coming."

"Shush!" Julianna blurted. "All right, all right. I'll keep quiet if you do."

"What's she talking about?" Benji asked. "Mac alluded to some sort of…what did he call it? A Charmageddon?"

Mali snorted, then said, "Looks like he got my sense of humor."

"And my good looks," Storm said, holding Daisy under her arms like an oversized ragdoll. "Anyone care to negotiate? Who's in charge here, Mali? You or your old man?"

Benji squinted, looking around Storm to see if he had any weapons. Daisy seemed to be unconscious, but her index finger was flicking as if she was tapping out a message. *Damn! It was probably Morse code but even if she knew it, he didn't. At least she was alive, clever, and willing to help.*

"Mali, do ye want to take on this brute, or shall I?" Benji asked, tipping his chin up to her to let her know he'd let her head the interrogation if she wanted.

She nodded in acceptance. Undaunted and with a gleam of hatred in her eye, Mali walked slowly around Storm, taking the lead and her time. She'd learned a little about intimidation from him over the years. He was impulsive and hated to wait, so that's what she'd make him do.

"Let's see, Da," she said with a smile in her voice. "You're about as tall as he is, probably stronger, too, since all Storm ever works is his jaw muscles."

"You're walking on thin ice, woman," Storm growled. "You know I can beat you, even with a hangover."

"You only ever tried with a hangover," she replied, still circling him, making him pivot in place to follow her. "But you're forgetting something very important…"

"What? And get on with it!"

"Why? Is that itty bitty girl getting heavy?" Mali laughed. "You're forgetting that you're now almost twenty years older than my father. He's both younger and in much better shape than you."

Storm glowered at her, following her movements, wary of her lunging unexpectedly to take his hostage from him. "That might be, but I have a hell of a lot more life experience than he does. And better equipment."

Mali glanced down at his crotch, taking the opportunity to look for what she was after. The shocker was in his left front pocket, a smallish bulge that may or may not have the safety switch set. She laughed. "I've taken what I want from you, Storm. All the best in you came out in one spurt. And that spurt's name is Mac."

His back straightened at the insult and his legs stilled, tired of dancing the waltz of words with his former paramour. "He was never meant to be. He is and always has been an accident."

Benji took advantage of Storm's distraction and reached out, pinching him hard in the muscle between his shoulder and neck, causing the man's legs to buckle. "He may be many things, but he's no accident. He's my grandson and here fer a reason."

Mac came in from behind the half-opened door and rudely shoved Storm – accidentally on purpose. "And if that reason is to neutralize your quest for chaos, all the better."

"It's not chaos," Storm hissed, his voice thin with pain, not quite a whimper. Hoping to get out of Benji's grasp, he dropped the inert girl in an unspoken compromise.

Free from his grasp, Daisy came to life. She paused, kicked the immobilized man in the shin, then scrambled to stand behind Jane. She straightened her hiked-up dress and stuck out her bottom lip, confident and secure.

"So, you think you have me, eh?" Storm asked, wincing at the new pain, stopped short of rubbing his leg by Benji's grasp.

Benji relaxed his grip and let him stand up. "Maybe."

Storm massaged his shin then sidled to the doorway and glanced at his opponents, gauging their strength and speed against his. It would be close, but he had the upper hand. He reached into his front pocket and gasped.

Gone!

"Looking for this?" Mac asked, holding up the orb. "You're slipping, old man."

Storm's eyebrows narrowed – Mac's shove hadn't been an insult but a theft – then relaxed. He could still negotiate. "Just give me my coins and I'll leave you alone. You'll never see me again. I promise."

"A promise from you is like a guarantee on tomorrow's price of gold," Mac said. "It depends on too many factors, one of them your integrity…which you don't have a molecule of. You're stuck here in 2015. Deal with it. Get a job, learn a trade. Hell, clean up some of the messes you created to help balance out your rotten karma."

"He won't," Mali said. "I hate to say it, son, but don't waste your breath. If it doesn't benefit him directly, he won't invest so much as a thought in it."

"She's right," Storm said. "I'll say one thing for your mother, she's the only one who 'got' me. Maybe that's why I kept her around for so long. How about it, Mali? Why don't we take a trip or two for old time's sake? Forward or back, your choice."

"Are you out of your mind?" Mali asked, her face skewed with disdain.

"Nope. If you don't want to join me, I'm sure I can talk another sweet young thing into it." He looked over at Daisy and smiled.

Daisy growled at him, then hid behind Jane again.

"I guess not her. I still have my charm, though."

"But no coins, right?" Mali asked.

He casually brushed the front of his other pocket, feeling for the reassurance of his last token, then blanched. He searched both sides but came out empty-handed.

Mali laughed out loud. "It wasn't me!" She looked up at Mac, one eyebrow raised.

Mac tossed the shocker in the air playfully, hoping to antagonize him more. "Nope, not me, either. All I took was this jewel."

"That bitch!" Storm yelled, lunging for the shocker.

Stepping to the side, Mac avoided contact, letting the angry Norseman stumble forward. Storm held onto the door and steadied himself, forehead furrowed as he thought of his options.

"Yup," Mac said, tossing the small orb again, "you're losing your balance, speed, and cleverness." He pivoted in place, watching Storm gather his wits. "I'd say you've run out of options, old man. Oh, and by the way…"

Storm grabbed for the immobilizer again.

This time, rather than move away, Mac stepped into the movement, shoving his shoulder into the tall, lanky man's gut, knocking the wind out of him, throwing him against the wall with the same blow.

The arc of Storm's toss was interrupted by the solid door, his fall slowed by the doorknob that bruised his spine as he slid down. Unintentional squeaks of pain slipped from his throat as he tumbled forward, "You were saying?" he asked, stalling for time to recover.

The shocker still in his hand, Mac brought out his phone, brandishing it with pride. "You were careless this round. Besides a cloud-ful of data including your book of contacts, bank accounts and other assets, dates, events, and casualties caused, you left a nice fat DNA sample at the house before you blew it up. Rather, before you sucked it into itself. According to those genomes, there's a long list of warrants – worldwide – out for your arrest. Your sweet little brag book ought to fill in a few spots without suspects, too."

"These cops can't do a damned thing. They got nothin'!"

"Ah, but they're not who you have to fear. Now the media has the man with no face. They have the jackal who's been thieving and creating chaos for decades without leaving a clue. They're going to love you. Not a minute's peace. They'll follow you everywhere. Jail would be heaven compared to the hell you'll be in when your anonymity is gone."

Sucking back his physical pain, Storm realized Mali's sister was the closest one to him. His only option for an escape was a hostage. Plus, she might have a coin. Time for the sympathy ploy. "Ouch, ouch, ouch!" he groaned as he stood up awkwardly, glancing at her to gauge the distance between them. *Come on. Move in closer to help a poor wounded man...*

"Don't!" Mali screeched, recognizing the look of tenderness in her sister's eyes. "He's a snake. A viper with a long reach!"

Heeding the warning, Julianna took two steps back into Silas's arms. Her retreat, however, had opened a path to the other two women in the room. Storm reached out, but Daisy had seen the glare of mischief and darted to Mac's side.

Jane turned around, confused at her charge's quick departure. Then she felt his sudden restraint, his hot breath on her cheek as he held her close, pinning her to him. "Ooh, I see where Mali gets her good looks," Storm whispered harshly. "Care to dump that big Scot and learn what a real man feels like?"

"She's my wife and verra pregnant," Benji growled.

Storm glanced down at her flat belly then back at Benji, not saying a word but one eyebrow raised.

"There really isn't such a thing as 'a little bit' pregnant, now is there?" Benji asked, slowly moving closer to the pair.

"Don't!" Storm hollered, glad that his strong voice had returned. He fumbled in his pocket for something – anything – as a prop. All he found was the rich old lady pickpocket's business card. He held it in the air as if it was a bomb. "All I need do is tear this and the whole house explodes!"

"Yer out of yer mind," Benji said caustically but with a glance to Mac to make sure Storm was bluffing. Mac shrugged minimally, unsure of what technology Storm could have brought back from the future.

"What is it you really want, Storm?" Mac asked. "You don't want a traveling companion, especially one who's pregnant with your former lover..."

Benji saw the glint of revulsion rise in the kidnapper's face and took over the interrogation. "And ye don't need a weapon because ye already have one…" he said, watching for his reaction.

Storm blinked back his twinkle of mischief. "What I want is my bag of coins. You know, the ancient silver drachmas so precisely drilled that with just a strong desire and the right portal, traveling to any time is possible."

The hint of pride at his ruse was seen by both Mac and Benji. The business card bomb was a dud, but he still had Jane. Neither MacKay male looked at the other. It was understood they'd take the first safe opportunity to grab her.

Noticing Mac and Benji's twin squints of confidence, Storm realized he'd blown it. They knew. She didn't, though – he could feel her shivers of terror. He didn't have long before they rushed him.

He needed a motorized getaway. Were the keys in the cars or hanging on the wall? He pulled her quivering body toward the doorway, then noticed the dartboard. He reached over and grabbed a fistful of the needle-pointed projectiles. "Don't even think of it, gentlemen," Storm snarled. He held the bundle to her neck, then down towards her womb.

"Which one? Do I kill Mali before she's born or ruin this baby maker so none of her brats get the chance to see daylight? Hmm? What will that do to your precious time-space continuum, Mali?"

Tweent! Tweent!

Benji and Mac rushed Storm at the car honking, but his reflexes were fast, too.

"Hold it!" Storm shouted as the rattle of darts hit the ground. Startled by the horn, he had dropped all but one. He kicked at them, scattering them across the parquet floor. He held the last one to Jane's neck, making a dent in her skin but not piercing it. "Looks like our ride's here. I don't know who it is, but one of you tell them to leave the car running and walk away. We'll be leaving now, right, sweetheart?"

Jane turned away from his nuzzle and gagged.

"Morning sickness or nerves?" Storm asked, his nose close to her ear. "Either way, get over it!"

He dragged her with him, walking backward, stumbling into a chair before reaching the door. "Open it slowly," he told Jane.

Her eyes flitted towards Benji, her surge of confidence making them bright with anger, not dull with fear. "I…I can't," she whimpered, her jaws clenched in rage.

Storm grunted with frustration. "Open it!"

"I…I can't," she repeated, her voice timid but her eyes now squinted, ready to attack.

"Damn it!" Storm brought his dart-holding hand down, grabbed the doorknob, and the door burst open, the surge of a heavy body knocking him to the wall.

Jane spun out of his grasp and stumbled towards Mac and Benji who quickly pulled her away.

Duchess snapped and snarled, then attacked Storm's upraised right arm, his blows now ineffective with the loss of his last weaponized toy.

"How…How…Who?" Silas asked as he watched the dog terrorize the kicking, flailing man, on the floor once again.

Julianna snuggled into her fiancé. "Hell if I know. Da, do you know whose car that is?"

"Get her off! Get her off!" Storm wailed, head thrashing side to side as she nipped at his nose.

"Nope. Never saw it before. Jane?" he asked coolly.

A short dark-haired woman walked into the room, sidestepping the feuding Duchess and Storm. "Hello, Julianna. Long time, no see."

"Ciara?" Julianna gasped.

"Ciara?" Storm echoed. "Get your damned dog off of me!"

"She's not my dog," Ciara said to him, then turned to Julianna. "How's the boy doing?"

Julianna walked up to her slowly, ignoring the melee by the door. She embraced her with both arms, snuggling her face into the much shorter woman's hair. "I thought you might be dead… His name is Oscar and he's great. Thank you so much for him."

Ciara pulled out of the hug and looked at Julianna, searching for sincerity. "I knew you'd be a good mother to him. I pop in every once in a while to see him. He doesn't know who I am but, my goodness, he really is a gem, isn't he?"

"Agh!" Storm screamed.

Silas stepped closer to the fracas and looked at the dueling duo. "Oh, quit whining. She's just playing with you. Hardly any blood." He snorted and added, "But it looks like one of you pissed your pants."

"Yes, officer, that man is a burglar, a thief, an arsonist, he kidnapped and threatened my wife, tried to force us off the road in what I suspect is a stolen car..." Benji enumerated the crimes on one hand, started on the next, then took a deep breath. "Oh, and my friend Silas Priest here is a private investigator. He...um...has access to DNA labs. According to him, you'd best keep this Storm fellow locked-up tight. It seems he's the culprit in quite a few unsolved crimes worldwide. DNA will out, right?"

"Silas Priest?" the policeman asked. "Is that him?" he nodded to Silas who was standing on the other side of the room, chatting with Ciara and Julianna.

"Yes, sir, it is. He's a little busy right now, though," Benji said.

"Oh, I've heard about him. He pretty much disappeared for the last four or five years. My uncle will be glad to hear he's back in action. Clever man."

"Aye, he is," Benji said. "Now, if ye don't need anything else from me, I'd like to check on my wife. She's a bit shaken, her bein' with child and all this excitement, ye ken."

"What about the dog? I hate to be a stickler, but if she's yours, you'd better get her shots and tags right away. We're pretty strict on that around here."

"Oh, Duchess is ours, all right," Benji said. "She's proved her worth more than once already. A better guard dog ye'll never find, no matter how many centuries ye search."

Chapter 21

"What do you want to do with these?" Silas asked, lifting the sunglasses out of the ice bucket.

"Storm's in prison and lost custody of them and I got everything I need," Mac said. "Take them with you to 2010. There might be something there that interests you."

"But I don't have a fancy phone or computer capable of accessing the information."

"How about an early wedding present?" Mac said. He handed him a paperback book-sized box. "I made a few modifications to a basic smartphone from Sprawl-Mart. It looks like any other one available, but it's a mini version of my 'genius' phone. It doesn't have all the same tools as mine but does have all the ones I used while here. Just hit star four-one-one to see the index of hidden apps. No one else will know."

"What about you, Mac? Have you decided what you're going to do?" Julianna asked.

Mali came in and grinned at him. "Or where or when you're headed?"

"I figure I'd stick around here for a few years. I have someone I'd like to get to know better…day by day. I don't want to skip any steps."

Mali hugged him around the shoulders, then kissed his cheek. "Yes, Daisy's a sweetheart. I've seen that look a lot lately."

"What look?" Mac asked.

Mali scowled at him. "I hope you're not that young and naïve, son. The look: the spark; the flare of passion contained; hope for a love everlasting; faith that it will arrive. All presented in a warm, moist structure capable of sharing physical bliss."

"Ew, Mom. I don't know whether to be impressed or disgusted."

"If it makes you feel more comfortable, I'm at the hope and faith stage. I never got the whole package. Now that I see Julianna and Silas, I know it's possible for me, too. It wasn't until I saw Mom and Da yesterday that I remembered how special it is. Or should be. As Da would say, 'Bide yer time. It will come.'"

Ciara knocked lightly on the door frame. "Where's that dog?" she asked. "I wanted to say goodbye to her before I left. She and I have been traveling companions for quite a while."

"How's that possible?" Mali asked.

"Don't know. I found her in 2008. With as much bouncing between eras, I knew I shouldn't form a bond. I didn't even give her a name: just called her Dog. Then four days ago, she followed me back to 1864. I didn't know that was even possible."

"What were you doing there?" Mac asked.

"I went there to dig up the stash I'd buried in the woods many years before. The spot was now next to the outdoor kitchen of a big plantation. Even with era-appropriate clothing, as a white woman, I couldn't be seen doing manual labor, especially with so many slaves around. I gave the woman we now know as Daisy an orange for digging it up for me.

"Once I had the bag and was ready to go, the dog walked away from me and sat down next to her. I figured she'd found her new home, so I said goodbye and left through the trees."

Jane added, "And when Daisy found the coin and was threatened by her boss, she ran through the trees, visualizing freedom, and she and the dog wound up here. Safe."

"Yup," Ciara said. "Storm's in prison with no chance for parole after all the laws he's broken and governments he's offended. I guess the prophecy came true: Red Storm was undone by his son. Mac got him busted."

"Were you looking for Duchess?" Daisy asked Ciara when she was done speaking.

"Oh, there you are, sweetie." Ciara ruffled the dog's freshly brushed hair. "Now, you be good for your new family. I think Miss Mali and I are going out to have some adventures, all right?"

"Gee, I guess this is a win-win-win situation," Mac said. "You get a permanent vacation with a good friend, and I get both the girl *and* the dog."

"Yup," Mali said. "A happy ever after on perpetual repeat."

The End

Thanks!

Thanks for reading Big Mac, the twelfth story in The Fairies Saga series.
Now that Ciara and Mali have a bag of time traveling coins, where are they headed? Or should that be, 'when' are they headed?
The future looks bright for Mac and Daisy, Benji and Jane, Silas and Julianna. Here's hoping Storm stays behind bars!
To find out more about how Benji and Jane met in the 18th century, read **The Great Big Fairy** (contains adult content).

About the Author

Author Dani Haviland started writing late in life and has been making up for lost time with a flood of works from sports, gritty tales, time travel, and Sweet and Sassy romances to Unforgettable romantic suspense, Cute But Crazy romantic comedies, and cozy mystery stories – with a couple of Short Sets thrown in to round out the reading experience.

Dani is also the owner of Chill Out! Books, one of the publishers for The Authors' Billboard. Follow her on Amazon and BookBub to make sure you get her latest stories.

Contact information:
www.danihaviland.com
Email: dani@danihaviland.com
Twitter: @dani_haviland, @gr8authors

I love to hear from readers!
Sign up for my newsletter to get the latest information on new releases, free stuff, and contests at: http://bit.ly/2DHnews

Awesome readers group!
I have a Facebook Page for folks who are interested in early excerpts and insights into my latest books and box sets. I'd appreciate a like on the page. Drop in and see if I've remembered to add photos and excerpts of my works in process. Search: Dani Haviland & Friends Readers Group.

Other Books by Dani Haviland

ARLIE UNDERCOVER SERIES (romantic suspense based in Alaska and Arizona)

A Stingray Christmas: (First book) Anchorage detective on medical leave travels from Alaska to Arizona to see for the first time the son he'd fathered as an anonymous sperm donor. Great and rotten surprises await the cop with the smartest smartphone around.

The Biggest Heart Ever: (Book two) When would Arlie learn that trying to do everything by himself could be deadly—and make Charlene a widow before they were married?

Always a Bigger Fish: (Book three) Back in Alaska, Arlie finds out he's a target. Will vacationing detective Billy Burke (from THE FAIRIES SAGA) have information to help nab the scalper?

How to Fix a Broken Life: (Book four) When Arlie's very pregnant wife is kidnapped by pseudo terrorists, will he be the one to rescue her or will a surprise hero come in to save the day?

Because You Said So: (Book five) Something's amiss at the Port of Anchorage. Will Arlie be able to solve it and still be back in time to wear the Santa suit?

THAT TWIN THING SERIES (romantic suspense series)

The Midwife's Son: The midwife refused her selfish patient's request to smother the scrawny twin and instead took him home to bring up as her own. Years later, will the two young men wind up in each other's lives despite the midwife's efforts to keep them apart?

Phoenix I'm Not: Will the billionaire's spoiled son be resurrected from the ashes of his former life of drugs and mayhem by love or be tortured and eliminated by the assassin sent by his mother?

Lost and Found Family: Separated at birth, these twins find they have more than genetics in common: they're both the target of killers who are willing to risk everything to take them out.

Peter Elph: A supplement to the story of Lost and Found Family, this short story is about a member of the Wagner family back in 1886 Tombstone, Arizona.

That Twin Thing: The Complete Collection: All four books in one place.

THE FAIRIES SAGA SERIES (historical fiction/time travel, listed in order with novellas):

Kibbles and Bits: FREE ebook: Sample the first stories in the series before you buy. The Fairies Saga stories. Find out how the first five books got their crazy names, too.

Naked in the Winter Wind: (lengthy novel) How does an older woman wind up as a young hottie in Revolutionary War era North Carolina? First book in the time travel series.

Ha'Penny Jenny: More about the naïve and psychic young girl who was adopted into a time traveling family. Will her past catch up to her?

Aye, I am a Fairy: (lengthy novel) Young British lord finds himself entwined with a time traveling family and must decide if he should go back in time, too. Second book in the series.

Dances Naked: (novel) Directionally challenged time traveler is rescued by Cherokee in 18th century. What must he do before the chief will show him to The Trees, the portal through time?

Chasing Christmas: A young Cherokee is rescued from an abusive man and changes the lives of many in this 18th century America family.

The Great Big Fairy: (lengthy novel) Very tall Benji grew up in the 20th century but was born in the 18th. When he finds a way to return to his grandparents in the distant past, he goes for it. Once there, he realizes he can't stay, but must return to the future. Fourth book in the series.

Little Bear and the Ladies: What's a bachelor trapper to do with all the females he rescues from the Hessian mercenaries? He'd better hurry and figure something!

Little Drummer Boy: Young Scout works to earn money for a home in post-Revolutionary War America but runs up against prejudices and snowstorms.

Never Too Young: Scout and Ha'Penny Jenny have grown up, but will they be able to spend their life together, or will the past and ruffians get in their way?

Time in a Little Blue Bottle: Elvis, Mark Twain, and the prime vampire are racing to get the bottle of Fountain of Youth water before sweet Bella and the youthful pickpocket. So why are time travelers Marty Melbourne and Master Simon interested?

Kidnapped!: Will Benji and his new brother-in-law be able to rescue his sister from one of the most inhospitable areas of Scotland?

CONTEMPORARY NOVELLAS – BENJI, THE LOST YEARS

Luke the Unexpected: Love of classic motorcycles brought them together, but Luke and Holly have other challenges to face. Find out how their friend Benji got his stripes here.

Pool Boy Wanted: No Experience Preferred: (rather racy) Young Benji has been a hostage and slave, but life gets worse when an older woman decides she wants him as her own.

STAND ALONE NOVELLAS (contemporary romances)

Kit Kringle: An Alaskan Tale: Kay moved to Alaska for the wrong reasons, then decided to stay and start her own business. What she hadn't planned on were prejudices and falling in love.

Be My Angel: Wyatt's dream to help save the wild mustangs began with the purchase of a rundown ranch in western Oregon. What he hadn't anticipated was being mesmerized by a sassy woman in a wheelchair.

Three Are One: The post chaplain tried to help the young widow adjust, but would his feelings for her and the search for his lost sister cause problems?

One Arctic Summer: That unforgettable summer of 1994 in Barrow, Alaska, and the touch she never forgot…If she goes back, will he remember her?

The Polar Xpress: Will the California chiropractor get a first chance at romance with the owner of Second Chance Kennels when he is stranded in Alaska?

Too Fast For You: Ten years after Little League, two talented professional baseball players wind up on the same minor league team. Will she remember him? And will their friendship be ruined if she does?

Coming Soon!
Triplets: Three Aren't One Series